Song of Phoenix and Ink

Margherita Scialla

paperback edition (black & white) - ISBN: 9798794139617
paperback edition (colored) - ISBN: 9798415356447

Story editing by Deb Nicholas
  ↳ www.languagesatwordswordswords.weebly.com
Cover art by Vasilisa // @padrebasil.art (twitter) @padrebasil (instagram)
Map art by Daniela A. Mera // @authordaniela.a.mera (ig & tiktok)
Characters art by Carman // @cchaiart (twitter & instagram)

to all the characters I have ever written about— and will write about in the future— whom I've hurt in any way:

~~I hope we never meet.~~
…..I'm so sorry for all the pain.

But at least I made you hot. That should make up for it.

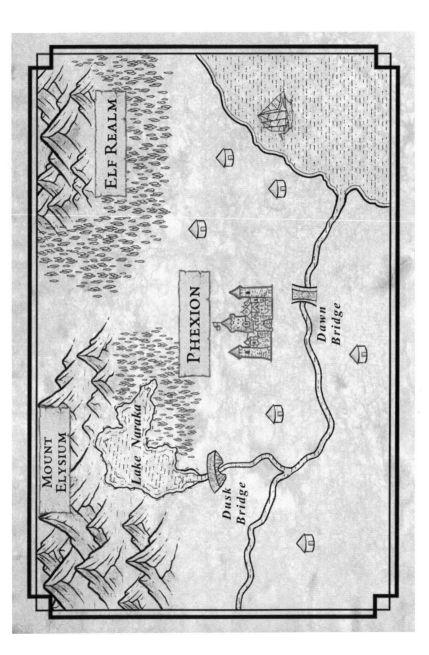

0.

Of all the things she could be doing on a Saturday morning, Nadzia had never thought she'd find herself staring at her reflection in a café window, whispering encouraging sentences to herself as if they were prayers.

From where she was standing she could see Sanna already sitting at a table, her eyes focused on the manuscript laying in front of her. Nadzia knew her friend well enough to understand that the frown on her face meant nothing good and couldn't help but grimace at the thought of all the things Sanna would soon be telling her. Nadzia knew Sanna was pretty critical about... well, everything. She was still her closest friend, though, and when she'd finally finished writing her book, after years of sweat and tears, Nadzia had wanted her to be the first to read it before anyone else did.

Nadzia stared into the brown eyes of her reflection and fixed her chestnuts curls one last time before taking a deep breath and pretending to be ready for what was awaiting her.

Nadzia entered the café. Sanna waved when she saw her, but her enthusiasm wasn't enough to calm Nadzia's slowly increasing anxiety.

"Hey," Nadzia said cautiously, slipping into the seat opposite her friend.

She was glad Sanna had at least chosen a table away from other people. If things didn't go well, she hoped no one would hear them argue. Thankfully the place was full enough for the chatter to make it hard to eavesdrop on others.

Sanna smiled. "I'm glad we could meet today. I've been wanting to talk about your book for days now."

"Yeah…" Nadzia forced a smile.

There's nothing to fear, she told herself. *It's only constructive criticism. You know she means well. Don't take it too seriously.*

Sanna straightened up and slowly slid the manuscript towards her friend.

"So…" She had literally only said one word and Nadzia already found herself on the edge of a breakdown. "There were a few things that I didn't really understand."

"Okay…"

"First of all, the title," Sanna started, "'*Crimson Mayhem*?' It sounds a little too theatrical and random for this type of story."

Nadzia shifted in her seat, trying to buy herself a few more seconds before she replied.

"Well, it's 'mayhem' because everything turns into chaos, and 'crimson' because of the blood from the massacre. And also because the villain, Malkiya, has red hair. Although that might be stretching it a bit far. I think it fits in the end."

Who was she fooling? She had spent years planning and writing this book and it was especially personal to her. No matter what she told herself, Nadzia was *not* ready to hear what was about to come out of her friend's mouth.

Sanna nodded, but the frown on her face didn't waver. "I understand your reasoning, but I still don't think it goes well with the story," she said. She then randomly changed the subject, as if her critique of the title was everything that needed to be said about the topic, without any room for discussion. "Why did you choose such difficult names? They're terribly hard to remember."

Nadzia was slowly getting defensive but hoped Sanna wouldn't be able to hear it in the strained tone of her voice.

"Well, if readers are used to names like Susan or James and don't want to make an effort to pronounce or remember the names I chose, then that's up to them," she argued. "The ones I chose aren't even difficult."

"You know how people are," Sanna continued, "If things are too hard they'll soon lose interest. If they don't know how to pronounce the names or constantly forget who's who, they won't even finish reading the story."

Nadzia clenched her fists under the table and reminded herself to stay calm. "That doesn't sound like my problem. If they can't put in a little effort and commit to a three hundred page book, then they shouldn't even start reading it in the first place."

Sanna sighed, annoyed by Nadzia's attitude, and slipped a hand through her platinum blond hair. Nadzia focused on the empty table behind her to try and calm herself down as her friend continued talking.

"Let's discuss all the creatures and places, then. You included many different things in this book, it feels so chaotic. Naraka is a term from Buddhism, right? You wanted to include that, which I totally understand, but then you use Elysium, which comes from Greek mythology. Can't you see it's all just a weird mix? Why do you even use mythology from our world if those countries and beliefs don't exist in your book?"

"It's a fantasy story, it doesn't need to be *that* logical!" Nadzia snapped.

"It needs to make sense to a certain extent," Sanna replied, equally fired up, "your world still needs to have rules."

The chatter around them only made Nadzia more worked up and the smell of coffee was starting to make her stomach turn.

"Everything I chose, the names, the creatures, have a meaning. I didn't create them randomly and the story wouldn't make sense if I changed all the things you're talking about." At this stage, Nadzia was simply trying to make up excuses to convince Sanna that her book was fine as it was. She didn't want to change the characters, she didn't want to change the geography of her fantasy world or the nature of the creatures in it. And she certainly didn't want to change the names or the title. She liked her book as it was and she wanted to leave it like that.

Nadzia had given her manuscript to her friend hoping for praise and words of encouragement, not a full on critical review. She should have expected it from Sanna, though, but still wished it hadn't happened.

"This book is never going to be successful," Sanna said eventually, "no publisher would actually publish it as it is. It might be different if you changed the things I suggested."

"I didn't write the book for other people to read, but for myself," Nadzia announced, defensively. She was only twenty-two. She was in no rush to become a published author and didn't care about fame or recognition. "If it gets published then that's great, but that isn't why I wrote it." Sanna opened her mouth to reply, but Nadzia was quick to continue. "If a publisher doesn't like the story and wants to change it? Traditional publishing isn't the only route. I can self publish just the way I want to, if I feel like it."

Nadzia shot up from her seat, the chair making a scraping sound as it moved back. Finally, she said, "I can do this even without your approval or support."

Without waiting for a reply, she grabbed her manuscript and walked out of the café.

Nadzia tried to reassure herself that her work was great, that Sanna was just being too critical, but no matter what she told herself, she couldn't help feeling hurt as her friend's words kept replaying in her head.

She slammed the door of her apartment behind her and furiously threw the manuscript on her desk. This situation wasn't new, it had happened many times before, but she still couldn't accept it. She understood Sanna was only trying to help, but it was the *tone* she used every time and all things she criticized when airing her views on topics about which she wasn't even an expert.

Nadzia sighed heavily and fell onto her bed, her arm covering her eyes. She could get angry at Sanna, but the real one to blame was herself. After all, she had given her friend the manuscript knowing full well how it would end.

She reached out to her nightstand to grab her earphones and closed her eyes again as her comfort playlist started.

Maybe a nap would make everything better.

1.

Nadzia wasn't completely awake yet, but her brain already sensed something strange.

When her mind had cleared a little, she realised she could hear birds tweeting. It might seem normal for some to wake up to such a sound, but it wasn't for her. She remembered going to sleep with her earphones in, although they might have fallen out while she'd moved around in her sleep.

The reason the sound seemed strange was that never, in all the years she had lived in that apartment in the city, had she woken up to birds singing. To car horns, maybe. To neighbors yelling at each other, also. But never to the type of calm silence disturbed by birdsong.

When she finally opened her eyes, annoyed by the noise, she saw green. Frozen in place she stared in front of her for a while, taking in her surroundings, the sound of birds and cicadas and the smell of grass and flowers around her.

After a few minutes of processing this, she started asking herself, "Am I still dreaming?"

It wasn't unusual for Nadzia to have vivid dreams, but she already knew while asking the question, that this wasn't a dream. She stood up, looked over herself quickly and was relieved to find she was still wearing the hoodie and sweatpants she had on when she went to bed.

Somewhere behind her a flock of birds flew away, probably scared by some sound or animal. She watched them until they disappeared out of sight.

She was standing in the middle of a field. Behind her she could see the beginning of a forest, whilst the field extended on either side. In front of her everything was still green, but she could glimpse shapes that looked like houses poking out from the side of a hill.

Nadzia weighed up her options. She couldn't stay here, but wandering into a forest probably wasn't a good idea either. Maybe if she found somebody, she could ask where she was and then, from there, figure out how she had ended up there and how to get home.

Sighing in frustration, she began her journey towards what she hoped was a town. But the distance was much greater than she had initially imagined.

The sun was shining brightly and although still high in the sky, it was slowly sinking on the horizon, telling her that it was afternoon. Nadzia cursed, first under her breath, then out loud since she was alone and no one would judge her. She wasn't athletic and considered herself to be quite lazy usually. Walking, especially aimlessly like this, was a pain in the ass. The fact that she was only wearing socks made her feet ache, and the sun on her head was making her even tireder and grumpier than she already was. It looked as if the town was getting farther away instead of closer.

When she finally saw the houses just a few kilometers from where she was, she almost collapsed in exhaustion and relief. Making one last effort she kept walking.

A farmer was working in a field just outside the town. He turned, surprised to see a girl on her own walking towards him from that direction, and looked Nadzia up and down, frowning at the way she was dressed.

"Ahm… hello," she said, not sure whether to approach him or not.

He looked up at her, raising an eyebrow in question.

"Could you tell me where I am?"

"You don't know where you are?" He asked in a condescending tone.

Nadzia bit her tongue to keep herself from talking back to him. "I got lost and I don't know where I am right now."

He looked annoyed that she was bothering him and keeping him from doing his work. "This is just a small village on the outskirts of Phexion," he said finally. Then he pointed to a road between two houses and continued, "That's the way into the village. You might want to look for a ride to the main city. You won't find anything else here."

He dismissed her and went back to his work, but Nadzia had already stopped listening to what he was saying after his first sentence.

Phexion.

There was no place with that name in the world she lived in —*the real world.*

But there *was* a Phexion in her story, the book she had spent years writing, the one she had been discussing with her friend the day before.

But it couldn't be *that* Phexion, could it? That world didn't exist, she had created it.

She took another look around, at the endless fields behind her, at the small houses she had in front of her, and the way the farmer was dressed. The scenery looked just as she had imagined when she had written the story.

The farmer had stopped working again to glare at her, silently telling her to go away. She mumbled an apology and walked towards the path leading into the town. She had never planned the small villages in detail, since the whole story took place in Phexion, on Mount Elysium or in fields, and the characters never actually travelled to the villages, but the old houses were, indeed, like the ones she'd imagined.

Since it was evening, people were going home, their expressions tired and their clothes dirty. The scent of freshly cooked meals emanated from different houses, making Nadzia's stomach growl in response.

Hungry and still in a state of shock, she tried to think of what to do. She didn't have any money to buy food for herself, and if this world really was the one in her book, then the currency wouldn't even be the same. She certainly couldn't knock on someone's door and ask them to feed her, but equally couldn't let herself starve. She wasn't used to skipping meals, and if she remembered correctly, she hadn't eaten since breakfast the day before. She could worry about where she was later. First, she needed food.

There was a pub at the end of the road she was walking along that was slowly getting more and more crowded with men wanting a few drinks after a hard day's work. Nadzia saw it as an opportunity. She couldn't pay for her food, but she could ask the owner of the pub if they would feed her if she helped them serve the customers that night. It was a fair exchange, surely they'd need some help with all the people that were walking into the tavern.

Nadzia felt a spark of excitement realizing she had some kind of a plan, even if it wasn't one that would get her home.

The smell of ale and freshly cooked sausage hit her as soon as she opened the door of the tavern. The place was large and to her left and right there were tables already filled with people drinking. Towards the end of the room on the right was the counter, with a stressed out barkeeper running around behind it. Next to the counter was the door to the kitchen, opened repeatedly by waiters trying to bring hot dishes to the tables. To the left of the room there were some stairs, probably leading to more tables.

Nadzia made her way over to the counter, hoping the poor barkeeper would give her a second of his time so she could make her proposal. She was almost at the counter when one of the guys sitting there stood up and turned around to leave. Nadzia froze at the sight of him, and he stopped in his tracks as well, suspicious of her reaction.

"Dacey..." she had said his name before she realized it. In her state of shock she didn't even notice whether he had heard her.

Nadzia just kept staring at him. Short, ruffled blond hair. Green eyes, wide open and staring at her distrustfully. The birthmark covering his temple and the space under his right eye made his olive skin slightly darker.

It was him.

It was the character she had created.

How was that possible?

As she stared at him in awe and surprise, he made a decision. Without giving her any more time to react, he grabbed her wrist and pulled her with him, dragging her up the stairs to the first floor of the pub. He opened a door and pushed Nadzia into the room, but before she could turn around or even say anything, something hit her on the head and then everything went black.

✳

Honestly, she should have expected it. If only she hadn't been so surprised by everything that was happening, she probably would have seen it coming. Nadzia was the one who had created him after all, she knew him better than anyone.

Of course Dacey would be suspicious. Being a shapeshifter, he used his abilities to his advantage to act as a spy on the king's behalf. He usually wore other people's faces, and no one could really tell which was his real one. Even the very few times he'd walked around wearing his real face, people couldn't be sure about it. Only the king's inner circle knew what his true form was. Well, the king's inner circle and Nadzia, of course.

So it shouldn't have come as a surprise he reacted that way when she recognized him while he was wearing his real face.

A splitting headache was the first thing Nadzia felt when she started coming to. She tried to bring a hand to her head but realized she couldn't move. When she opened her eyes, her sight fell onto Dacey, sitting on a table right in front of her.

He glared at her as she looked around the empty room, and then down at herself, confirming she was indeed tied to a chair. She sighed in defeat.

"I'm going to ask you some questions, and you're going to answer me truthfully," he started. "I think you can already predict what will happen if you don't."

"I'll die?" She asked. She already knew, but asked anyway just to buy herself time to come up with something else to say.

"Good guess."

"And there I was hoping we were going to become friends."

"Sarcasm won't get you anywhere," he replied.

Nadzia raised an eyebrow, challenging him to start with the questions.

"Who are you?"

"I'm no one," she answered. She felt some sort of childish joy at her own reply. Maybe the shock of the situation she found herself in was messing with her head.

"I'll ask again," he said in a low voice, leaning towards her, "who are you?"

"I'm literally no one important. I'm not even supposed to exist in this world." Not the answer he wanted, but it wasn't a lie.

With a swift motion he grabbed a sword that was lying on the table behind him and pointed it at her. He was close enough to be able to angle the sword so that its point was almost touching her neck without even having to get up from his seat. His eyes showed just how annoyed he was.

"You already know how this will end, and you still don't want to cooperate. Are you not afraid of death?"

"I'm terrified, actually" Nadzia replied, her tone serious and quiet for the first time since they had started the conversation. He noticed the change, too, but didn't lower his sword.

"Let's try again," he said, "how do you know me?"

In a moment of weakness and hoping that the truth would actually work, she said "I created you."

This seemed to surprise him and he was taken aback for a few seconds. Nadzia was sure he was trying to come up with a reply, but before he could actually respond there was a knock on the door. Dacey stood up and put the sword back on the table. He walked out of the room, but was close enough when he talked to whoever it was that had interrupted them, that Nadzia heard most of their conversation.

"She knows who I am, which is pretty much impossible, and she keeps saying weird things. Maybe she's crazy. I think we should let Lucjan deal with her."

"Are you sure it's safe to take her to the city, and even more so, to the king?"

"She seems to be a regular human being. She could only do us harm if she managed to leave Phexion after meeting with the king, but that will probably never happen."

"Alright, just bring her downstairs. The carriage is ready."

The door opened again and Dacey walked back in with a black cloth in his hand.

"You're coming with us," he said, blindfolding her. He untied her from the chair and fastened metal cuffs around her wrists. Holding her by the arm, he guided her down the stairs and then outside, where he helped her climb into a carriage, then attached the cuffs to the floor.

Sitting in the dark, all she could do was listen to the horses, trying not to get an upset stomach as they started their journey.

NAME: Nadzia Kaminski
HEIGHT: 166 cm / 5'5"
AGE: 22
HAIR COLOR: chestnut brown
EYE COLOR: brown
ENTITY: human

2.

Nadzia wasn't completely sure how long they had been traveling, but it had to be a full day already. Her stomach was growling so loudly that it even drowned out her headache. When the carriage stopped she wasn't expecting anything to happen but tensed when she heard the door open. A hand took her blindfold off and she blinked so her eyes would adjust to the sudden change.

Dacey was sitting in front of her with a loaf of bread in his hand. Nadzia eyed the bread hopefully. She wanted to reach out and grab it, but stopped herself, looking up at the young man again. He didn't give any sign of wanting to give her the food.

"Is this the next level of torture? You starve me until I say what you want to hear?" Dacey kept looking at her, not saying a word. Nadzia bit her lip, her stomach starting to growl again. She closed her eyes and sighed in defeat. "I haven't eaten in two days at least," she said quietly, "Please."

He took a key out of his pocket and removed the handcuffs. She quickly grabbed the loaf from his hand before he could even try to give it to her. He seemed taken aback for a moment, then leaned against the side of the carriage and relaxed as he watched her eat it all. He noticed her disappointment when she finished it and realized it wasn't enough to calm her hunger.

"Can I… can I have some more?" She asked, cautiously, avoiding eye contact.

"Will you cooperate if I bring you more?"

Nadzia rolled her eyes. "I don't know what you expect to hear from me. I'm not a spy or an enemy, I have done nothing wrong and I surely didn't mean to end up here. I just want to go home."

"Where's *home*, exactly?"

She thought about it but didn't have a reasonable answer. She was sure she still hadn't entirely processed where she was or what was going on.

"I don't know," she whispered. He frowned at her but she ignored him.

She forcibly shook her head to rid herself of the bad thoughts, telling herself to focus on where she was. She sat up straighter and finally looked back at him. "Am I at least allowed to get out of here to relieve myself? I've been in here for quite a while and since it seems I'll have to spend more time in here, I'd rather keep it clean."

He grimaced at the image she'd planted in his mind, and she almost grinned at that reaction. Finally he let her out of the carriage and she did what she had to. When she was escorted back into the carriage by the guards, she found a glass of water and another loaf of bread waiting for her. They locked her back into her personal prison, but this time didn't handcuff or blindfold her.

After they set off on their journey again, Nadzia got up and looked out of the little window in the door. Trees framed the road, and guards and knights rode on horses behind her carriage.

A guy on one of the closest horses caught her attention and she couldn't help but stare, even when he looked back at her. She was already aware that warm brown eyes and freckles were a killing combination for her, and seeing them for real instead of in her imagination confirmed it.

She took in every detail. The shoulder length black hair and the two braids along one side of his neck. She marveled at his dark, sun-kissed skin and the little mole under his right eye. His appearance and the fact that he was traveling with Dacey told her enough about who he was.

Xayvion kept looking straight at her, expression blank and calm and never changing, even when she smiled softly at him. They kept traveling for hours, but their eyes never left each other.

Nadzia couldn't explain it, but Xayvion's eyes calmed her. He had been one of her favorite characters when she'd first written the story and somehow he looked even more comforting and beautiful than she had imagined. She had created him to be kind, so it made her feel he could possibly be her key to get out of the predicament in which she found herself.

Around them, the trees had been replaced with houses and shops. The roads were wider and busier, and some of the people stopped to look at the procession, curious to get a peek of who or what was inside the carriage.

When they finally stopped, she stepped back from the door and waited for it to open. Dacey was the one that came to get her and he made sure to put the handcuffs and blindfold on again.

"Really? The blindfold too?" She asked, irritatedly.

"We can't let you know what the inside of the castle looks like, now can we?"

Nadzia held back a laugh. She didn't need to see it to know what the castle looked like. She already knew almost every single hallway and secret passage in it.

Holding her by the arm, Dacey guided her into the castle to the room where she would meet the king. They walked for a long while and she was pretty sure he was trying to confuse her by taking detours. Nadzia found it amusing how hard he was trying.

Finally, they entered a room and Dacey made her sit on a chair, connecting her cuffs to a chain attached to the floor. When the blindfold came off, the first thing her eyes landed on was the figure of King Lucjan. She found herself unconsciously holding her breath at the sight of him. Tall, broad and muscular. Dark brown skin, brown hair and brown eyes. A sight to behold. Even the scar on the left side of his face looked attractive. She mentally gave herself a pat on the back for creating him like that.

"Do you stare at all the people you encounter?"

The voice brought her back to reality, her eyes meeting Xayvion's. She wasn't surprised he was there as well, being the king's right hand man and closest friend, but was still happy to see him again.

Nadzia quickly looked around and realized they were in the king's meeting room. The big table where he usually sat to talk about the city's affairs with his inner circle was right behind her. In front of her stood the king, with Dacey and Xayvion on either side.

"Now *that's* a nice sight," she mumbled to herself, grinning.

Dacey raised an eyebrow at her, as if to say '*Really?*'.

Lucjan turned his head slightly towards Dacey, but his eyes never left her. "Brief me," he ordered.

"I met her at the Golden Fields Pub," he started, "She knew who I was as soon as she saw me. She specifically said my name."

"Are you sure you've never met her before?"

"More than sure," Dacey confirmed.

Lucjan finally focused his attention solely on her, quickly checking her from head to toe to see if there was anything suspicious about her appearance.

He frowned. "Why are you dressed like that?"

Nadzia had forgotten she was still in a hoodie and sweatpants. And grass stained socks.

"It's what I wear when I sleep," she replied quietly, embarrassed. He looked confused, but let it slip as it wasn't relevant for the moment.

"Who are you?" He asked, finally.

Nadzia held herself back from sighing in frustration. "I'm no one. Just an irrelevant human."

"Does the irrelevant human have a name?"

She held his gaze for a few seconds, debating whether she should say it or not. She didn't want to tell him too much about herself, but the more she lied or refused to tell them something, the more suspicious they'd get, and she had less of a chance of going home. Maybe being completely honest was the only way to earn their trust.

"Nadzia," she said in the end. "Nadzia Kaminski."

"So, tell me Nadzia," Lucjan continued, "what were you doing at that pub?"

"I was hungry and wanted to eat."

"You had no money on you," Dacey interrupted, "no other possessions, either."

"Thanks for publicly shaming me for being broke." She rolled her eyes, then glared at him. "I wanted to offer to work for them in exchange for food."

"Let's pretend that's true for a minute," the king said, annoyed. "How do you know him?"

She bit her lip, anxiously. Yes, she decided just to tell the truth, but it wasn't going to be easy. Her story sounded ridiculous. No one would believe her.

Finally, she said, "I created him."

A confused silence followed.

"You what?" Lucjan asked.

"I created him, and you, and this city and this whole world you live in," she said.

He looked to the left at his friend. "Is she telling the truth?"

"For the millionth time, I'm not a lie detector," Xayvion retorted rolling his eyes, annoyed, "but she does seem to be telling the truth. I don't feel anything suspicious."

Before they could ask her any other questions, she continued. "This world isn't real and neither are you. Well, now that I'm in it, it feels pretty real, but it didn't exist before I started creating it. You are characters in a story. I chose your names, the way you look, your backgrounds, whether you would be villains or heroes. You think you own your lives but they were actually all chosen and molded by someone else."

The silence continued as they mulled over the possibility of what she had just told them. Maybe dropping all that information on them at once hadn't been a good idea. Maybe she should have phrased it a little better, sugarcoated the truth to make it sound less brutal.

"You want us to believe there's a Supreme Being writing all of our destinies?" Xayvion said, in disbelief.

"Yes. Quite literally."

Nadzia found it a little funny that he would phrase the question like that when he already knew that gods existed in this world. But then again, said gods had a complicated relationship with people's lives.

"Is that supposed to be a metaphor?" Dacey asked, confused.

"I wish it were as simple as that," she replied, looking dejected.

Xayvion and Dacey glanced at each other.

"Now I understand what you were saying," Xayvion told him.

Nadzia looked at both of them and scoffed in disbelief. She remembered Dacey calling her crazy when he was talking to someone outside that room at the pub. That man must have been Xayvion.

"Sure, go on, continue talking as if I'm not right in front of you and have no idea what you're insinuating."

The two of them turned their focus on her but their expressions betrayed no emotion.

Lucjan completely ignored what she'd just said. "If this world is inside a story you created, how are you in it, too?"

"Finally someone asking a real question," she said, sarcastically. "If you find the answer do tell me, because I'm lost, too."

"What makes you think we'll believe you?"

Nadzia thought about it for a while. Telling them things no one's supposed to know would help her prove her point, but it would also make them think she were a spy, even more than they already did.

She held her head high and looked Lucjan straight in the eye. "This room is your personal meeting room. Not the public one where you talk with generals and politicians, but the one you use to plan things with your inner circle of trusted people. We're in the north wing of the castle, fourth door on the right, second floor." She gestured with her head to Dacey and continued. "He's a shapeshifter. He can change everything about himself and turn his features into any he wishes to have. He could turn into an animal too if he wanted, but he rarely does so since he doesn't like the way it feels."

Then, she looked at Xayvion. "Your name is Xayvion. You're an empath, you can feel people's emotions. Actually, to be more precise, depending on what they're feeling and its intensity, you can *see, feel, smell* and *taste* their emotions. That's why Lucjan wants you to be present during interrogations. You might not be a lie detector, but emotions say a lot about a person, especially in this kind of situation."

She stopped for a second to really look at them and, even if they were trying to mask their feelings, she could see all three of them were concerned and surprised that she knew so much.

She looked at Lucjan again.

"You're a king now, but you used to be a deity of war. Not the kind of god people prayed to when they wanted to win a battle, but the kind that was supposed to protect soldiers and civilians during war. The upper realms deemed you unworthy and banished you, forcing you to live in exile amongst the humans and all the other mythical creatures that live in this world." She raised an eyebrow at Lucjan questioningly. "Do I need to say more, or is this enough?"

Even though the things she'd stated about Dacey and Xayvion were well kept secrets, they might possibly be something a really good spy could find out. But not even the inner circle knew much about Lucjan. He did trust them with his life, but also kept many details from them so as not to put them in danger. Nadzia hadn't exposed anything private, but she gleaned she'd delivered a clear message that she knew more about him.

"You do know quite a lot," Lucjan said finally. "What do you want?"

Nadzia almost scoffed. "You ask that as if I'm blackmailing you into doing something I want."

"You're not?"

"I'm not. I only gave you the information to prove a point, not to threaten you. Sharing it with anyone else wouldn't benefit me in any way at all," she explained. They were the heroes of her book, the good guys. She couldn't exactly go ask the villains for help, so of course she couldn't use her knowledge in any other way. "All I want to do is find out why I am here and how I can go back to my world. I didn't even want to come here, but *you* brought me to the castle with you."

"For obvious reasons..." Dacey mumbled, which earned him a glare from her.

"While the things you said about us make a lot of sense, your story doesn't," the king offered.

"You live in a world full of magic, a world where underworlds and heavenly realms exist. Why is it so hard for you to believe there are other worlds out there, too?"

Lucjan held her stare in silence. He didn't look troubled by her question, but he didn't reply or give away any kind of reaction either.

"Xayvion, you should take her to her cell," Lucjan ordered, "Dacey you stay here, I need to discuss something with you."

Both of them nodded, and Dacey took a step towards his friend, handing him the blindfold. Lucjan snatched it before Xayvion could take it. "Don't bother with this, she clearly already knows where she is and where she's going to go."

Dacey looked a little embarrassed since he hadn't thought of that.

Nadzia just watched in silence as Xayvion grabbed her chains and guided her out of the room. She felt like a dog being taken for a walk, but she held back her snappy comment.

"You really don't believe me, do you?" She asked when they were almost at the underground prison.

"Your story doesn't sound very believable," he commented simply.

"You checked my emotions the first time I saw you from the carriage, didn't you? I already knew who you were then," she started. "Tell me, what did you feel from me?"

His silence told her enough. She insisted. "What did you feel from me?"

"Happiness," he gave in, his voice low.

The underground part of the castle was cold and surprisingly deserted. All the cells were empty, and the only sign of life were the two guards standing in front of the door.

"If I were a spy, or the enemy in general, and were here to lie to you, why would I feel happiness at seeing you? You know the emotions you feel are real. You've tested your abilities many times and you know the feelings you feel don't lie." He opened the door to her cell and gently pushed her inside.

"Yes, that part doesn't make sense to me either, but I know there's a logical explanation to all of this, and I'll make sure I find it."

The door closed, separating Nadzia from him. Without another word, he turned and walked away, leaving her standing in the middle of her cold cell, feeling miserable and exhausted.

3.

The wall to her left and the ceiling were both grey stone, with hints of mold in the corners. The bars of her cell were rusty and covered three sides so she could see into the other cells, which all looked the same apart from the fact that, unlike hers, they were empty. Despite the open space, the air felt stuffy.

She missed the convenience of watches. She couldn't imagine what time it was at all.

She had created the prison as a rusty old place that made prisoners think they were hopelessly lost, but if she had had any idea that she would end up in the same place one day, she would have made it nicer. The empty, creepy surroundings didn't give her the chance to close her eyes even once during the night. Nor did the figures of the two guards standing as still as statues either side of the door make it easier. They looked especially creepy in the darkness of the night. Without even a candle to light the place, the only source of light was the moon streaming in through the small windows high up on the walls.

Nadzia kept staring at the ceiling, lost in thought.

Was she actually in her own book? If things had gone a little differently, she would have been ecstatic.

She had seen the scenery and met the characters she'd created, but it still didn't feel real. Everything that had happened over the previous couple of days made her feel apathetic.

She sat up and leaned against the cold wall, taking a deep breath before she started to recap her situation.

She was inside the book she had written. That seemed to be a fact, even if her brain still hadn't acknowledged it.

Nadzia had no idea how she'd got into it, nor how she could get out. *Yet.*

She had met Dacey, Xayvion and Lucjan, meaning just two other main characters were left. Was she going to meet them soon?

She had been imprisoned by her characters... betrayed by her own creations... It felt weird, but she couldn't explain what it felt like other than that. She wasn't even sure *what* she was feeling at the moment.

A thought suddenly came to mind.

When, in the story, was she? Had the war already happened? She hadn't paid attention during the journey to notice details about the roads and villages. In her original manuscript, all her main characters had survived the war without any new or noticeable scars so she couldn't rely on their appearance to figure it out.

Nadzia closed her eyes, praying that she had appeared at a time of peace. She would *not* be able to survive otherwise.

The sound of footsteps pulled her away from her thoughts. Xayvion appeared in front of her cell and opened the door.

"Time to walk the dog?" She asked, grinning.

He grimaced and gestured for her to come out of the cell. Apparently he didn't like the joke. She shrugged and got up. He started walking as soon as she stepped out and she froze for a second, confused.

"You're not putting handcuffs on me today?"

He stopped to look at her and said, "You're just a human, what could you ever do?"

"Ouch." She rolled her eyes.

He started walking again and Nadzia followed him, nodding a greeting to the guards by the door who didn't even look her way. She felt Xayvion's eyes on her.

"You're acting weird," he said.

"Sleep deprivation and traumatic experiences do that to a person," she replied, nonchalantly, "This whole situation has enabled me to check both off my list."

He kept looking at her while they walked, his expression focused and serious.

"You don't need to stare at me like that to feel my emotions," she said. "What's making you so uncomfortable?"

"If what you say is true, that you're just human and have suddenly appeared in a world that's different to yours, why are you so calm? Shouldn't you be worried?"

"I don't think I've actually processed it. Or maybe I've already lost it and can't feel anything anymore," she explained. "I can't tell which of the two it is."

He shook his head, a disappointed look on his face. He'd clearly expected another type of answer but Nadzia couldn't tell what he'd wanted to hear.

They walked into the meeting room, where Lucjan and Dacey were already waiting for them. The king gestured for Nadzia to sit. Eyeing the single chair in the middle of the room suspiciously, she decided to just go sit on it. At least they hadn't tied her up or handcuffed her this time around.

"Let me guess, you'll ask me the same questions as yesterday but expect me to give you different answers," she said before they'd even started.

King Lucjan's stare hardened and she panicked slightly, momentarily worried she'd crossed the line.

"You're in no position to be acting so brazen," he started, his voice low, "I don't *need* you, so if you don't answer properly or you piss me off, I can just get rid of you. Simple as that."

Nadzia couldn't find a reply. Admittedly, she realized it was better if she kept her mouth shut. She did want to go home in one piece after all.

"We're doing some research about you, but while we wait, why don't you tell us about yourself again?"

Nadzia repressed the urge to roll her eyes. "Even if you try to dig up info about me, you won't find anything. I'm…" She found herself throwing her hands around crazily, "new to this world."

Lucjan scoffed. "You're a little too old to have just been born," he replied jokingly.

"I wasn't born, I just… appeared?" It didn't make sense to her either, but how could she even explain it? She really felt like she was digging her own grave.

"Right, because you're from another world."

"Yes," she said, a little too enthusiastically, ignoring the sarcasm in his statement.

Lucjan sighed deeply and ran a hand through his brown hair.

"So, what you told us yesterday is that you're human, that you wrote a story and that *somehow* you have appeared in it," he summarized.

She felt exhausted. "Yes."

"And if we are only the characters you created, it means that we are not real," he continued.

He wasn't trying to understand it. He was trying to make her repeat the story until she gave herself away with some secret or other. But Nadzia didn't have any secrets he could benefit from.

"You are, in fact, not real," she answered, trying to stay calm. "You are a figment of my imagination."

The more he asked, the more she got upset. The more she had to repeat herself, the more her patience ran out.

"If that's true then how did you end up here?" Lucjan asked again.

"I already said I have no idea!" She snapped.

A deafening silence followed her outburst. Even Dacey and Xayvion, who had listened to everything without talking or showing any kind of reaction, were now glaring harshly at her. She swallowed and could almost hear her heartbeat echo around the room.

"I'm sorry, I didn't mean to shout," she said, quietly. "I get that you don't believe a single thing I've said, but pretend for a moment that you do. I was dragged away from my world without warning and magically dropped here, in a world that I only know theoretically. I don't know how I got here, I don't know how to go back, and I don't know what to do to make

41

you understand that I'm *scared* and that I didn't want any of this to happen in the first place."

Her voice broke and she felt hot tears behind her eyes, but she almost felt relieved by her reaction. It was the first real emotion she'd shown since she'd found herself in this world. It was the first time she'd actually *felt* something since she'd found herself in this situation.

Only Xayvion's expression softened a bit, and she could tell he was feeling just how desperate and lost she was.

"Can you just tell me what you want from me?" She asked, weakly. "I don't think I'll be able to handle this much longer."

While writing her book, she always used to say that her characters felt like they were her babies. She had created them and she loved them just the way they were. She had never thought she could despise them this much.

"I just want to understand how you know so much about us," Lucjan answered.

Nadzia felt she was becoming hysterical. "But I—" She stopped for a second when her voice broke again, "I already told you… at least five times already."

"What you're asking us to believe is impossible."

"Just because you've never heard of it before, it doesn't mean it can't happen," she replied. Trying to keep herself from raising her voice was getting hard. "You live in a world full of magic, why is it so hard for you just to *believe*?"

"We live in difficult times, we can't trust what anybody says," he replied, his voice softening a bit, surprising Nadzia.

A heartbeat later, she realized what he had just said.

"Has the war already happened?" She blurted out.

The three of them looked at each other, taken back.

"War?" Xayvion asked.

Nadzia's eyes widened at the realization that she might have just told them something about their own life that they probably weren't supposed to know. She bit her lip and told herself to calm down, to think before she spoke again.

"What I meant to say was... What season of the year are we in?" She tried again.

"Early spring," the king replied.

She grimaced. "Oh, no."

Of all the times she could have appeared in the story, why did it have to be before all the disasters happened? She couldn't survive a war in a magic world!

"What is it that you're not telling us?"

Nadzia avoided any possible eye contact with them, trying to come up with an excuse or something to say. Would telling them the truth be a good thing? Maybe if she told them what Malkiya was going to do, they would finally consider her an ally. But what if they didn't believe her? What if, for them, it offered more proof that she was an enemy?

"I'm waiting..."

She looked up at Lucjan. "You know how I said I'm the author of this story? Well, I happen to know what the other characters are doing as well. I know you're currently worried about what is going on around the area of Lake Naraka. You've received complaints from villagers and heard stories of monsters, so you sent Hedyah with a group of soldiers to investigate."

Lucjan straightened after hearing the name of his knight and, again, looked at Nadzia suspiciously.

"I can tell you who is causing trouble and what they are doing before you even receive a report from her," she stated.

"Enlighten me, then," he challenged her.

"I believe I only need to say one name," she replied, feeling a little theatrical. "Malkiya."

She saw all three men flinch and then freeze, as if time had stood still. She looked at them dramatically, one by one, feeling strangely powerful.

"He's back and living on Mount Elysium," she said. "He's doing experiments and summoning beasts to the lake in preparation for war."

She stared straight into Lucjan's eyes in silence for a few seconds. "He's coming for you."

"For me, specifically?" He asked, his voice slightly strained.

"For you, and for the kingdom you rule," she explained. "He can't stand that you managed to build yourself a place like this after you were banished. He's jealous because you're a king and he's no one, forced to live in exile with monsters. He wants to get rid of you, get rid of all the people he considers weak." She leaned back in her chair, feeling smug. "He plans to sit on your throne."

"The upper realms won't let that happen," Lucjan tried to reason.

Nadzia scoffed. "The upper realms don't care. They don't care about a fallen god, and they especially don't care about the common folk. *You* should know that better than anyone."

She saw the realization in his eyes.

"He corrupted himself, didn't he?" He asked, eventually.

Nadia nodded. "He's a ghoul now."

Lucjan closed his eyes, forcing himself to hold it together.

"He used to talk of the procedure all the time," he confessed, "it's one of the reasons why they banned him."

She didn't want to give him time to process the information and come to a conclusion of his own, so she started talking again.

"I know some things about him, and what he plans to do. I could tell you everything I know. All I want in exchange is not to be treated like a criminal."

He opened his mouth to reply, probably to say something mildly threatening to put her back in her place, but then he closed it without saying anything.

After a while, he announced, "You'll go back to your cell for today. Hedyah is supposed to be back in two days. If her information aligns with yours, I'll consider your offer."

NAME: Dacey

HEIGHT: 170 cm / 5'7"

AGE: 22

HAIR COLOR: blond

EYE COLOR: green

ENTITY: shapeshifter,
born human

4.

The next two days passed very slowly, the minutes morphed into an endless loop of *nothing*. Outside it must have been cloudy, since even when it was supposed to be day, almost no light came in through the small windows.

Nadzia's meals were brought to her by the guards, who refused to interact with her whenever she tried to talk to them. No one came by during those two days, leaving her alone with her thoughts and the two guards who were very much like statues.

Her head still felt weird. She had so many chaotic thoughts that they drowned each other out, almost making her feel as if there weren't a single thought at all. So many things at once made her feel empty instead of full. *It felt odd*.

Since no one wanted to indulge her with idle chat, she ended up singing any pop songs that came to mind, trying to pass the time by coming up with what shapes the mold on the ceiling looked like.

When she heard footsteps approaching, it took her a moment to recognize they were lighter than Xayvion's, and a different rhythm to Dacey's. Her heart knew who it was before she even came through the door of the dungeon. Nadzia felt herself choke up when she saw her.

She stared in awe and fear as Hedyah calmly stopped in front of the door of her cell. She had clearly just arrived at the castle because she was still wearing her armor, which wrapped perfectly around her generous curves. Hedyah tilted her head, openly judging Nadzia's appearance, but Nadzia was too mesmerized by her beauty to care. She couldn't even find her voice to speak.

Hedyah's skeptical tone brought her back to reality. "You're the crazy prisoner Dacey brought back?"

"Aye," Nadzia replied, holding back a grin.

"I heard the stories you told the king," she said. "Did you really think anyone would believe you? Making up lies and digging up someone's past is nothing brilliant, anyone could do it."

"I'm not lying," Nadzia stated.

"Entertain me then," she said, a wicked smile on her face, "tell me something about myself that no one knows."

It was too good an opportunity for Nadzia to waste. She knew she would be digging her own grave, but all she could think about was that it would be worth it. She'd always wished to meet Hedyah and tease her personally.

"You took Faleece with you on the mission, didn't you? You should just tell people you're together instead of making her sneak in and out of your tent at night."

Nadzia witnessed the moment Hedyah's anger took over. The door of her cell was thrown open, hinges flying, and in a second Nadzia's back hit the wall, Hedyah's face was close to hers, her dagger lightly scratching her neck. At five foot ten, she towered over Nadzia. A few strands of red hair fell over her unnaturally blue eyes, which were literally shooting lasers.

"How do you know," Hedyah hissed in a low voice.

Nadzia's gaze fell on the scars on her face, contrasting with her pale complexion, then further down to her lips. She shook her head. *You need to calm down*, she told herself. *You gave her a girlfriend, so keep your hands and thoughts to yourself.*

"If you'd heard what I said over the past few days you'd already know the answer to that," Nadzia replied, trying to move her neck away from the blade.

They stared into each other's eyes. Hedyah was breathing heavily and Nadzia wasn't sure if she was trying to calm down, or building up her anger before she actually cut her throat.

Nadzia broke the connection long enough to glance at the two guards, who were still standing by the door.

"Aren't you guys also supposed to keep me safe?" She asked, nervously.

For the first time, one of them spoke. "Never had that order."

Nadzia's mouth fell open. *Assholes.*

Hedyah gave her a final push towards the wall and let her go, backing off but not putting the dagger away, as if waiting for another comment to provide an excuse to kill her.

"Hurry up and follow me," she snapped. "The king's waiting."

Hedyah walked off and Nadzia hurried after her. She made sure she kept close enough so Hedyah wouldn't complain, but still far enough so she could back away to safety if needed. She enjoyed playing with fire, but only to a certain extent.

When they walked into the meeting room, Nadzia noticed that other than the three men, Faleece was also there. She, too, looked more beautiful than Nadzia had imagined. Her thin grey eyes studied Nadzia carefully, and Nadzia gazed back as a challenge to look deeper.

Hedyah shot Nadzia a glare as a warning not to make any comment about her girlfriend in front of other people.

"Since everyone is finally here, let's start," Lucjan said.

Nadzia felt a pair of eyes on her and looked up to find Xayvion staring at her neck with a confused expression. Her eyes widened slightly and she brought a hand to her neck, seeing it come away with a few drops of blood. Hedyah must have pressed harder than she had realized. Or maybe the blade had just been *really* sharp.

Thankfully no one other than Xayvion seemed to have noticed, or cared.

"We're ready to hear your report, Hedyah."

Hedyah straightened. "We've been to the villages that reported attacks, all of them said the beasts were wrapped in dark mist. They attacked during the night and unfortunately the ones who survived weren't able to describe what they looked like. Most of them weren't able to get a proper look at the creatures, either." Lucjan nodded for her to go on. "The villagers said that the beasts came from and then returned in the same direction: Lake Naraka. We went there to check the situation and found a barrier of black mist right outside the forest. We tried to walk past it but it pushed us back with some kind of lightning shock."

51

Nadzia had to hold herself back from laughing. The fact that they didn't know the world electricity was strangely hilarious.

"We went back and walked to the other side of the Dusk Bridge—"

"I told you not to go over that bridge," Lucjan cut her off.

"I know, but this matter is way more serious than you think, and that was our only way of actually finding out what was going on," she replied. Her expression became troubled. "We saw something. Someone."

Nadzia saw Lucjan preparing himself to hear the name again.

"Malkiya is alive, and he's on Mount Elysium," Hedyah announced. "He's putting an army together."

The king was less surprised than the first time he'd heard it two days earlier, but his expression was still troubled. His eyes slowly went to Nadzia.

"I told you so," she replied, quietly.

Hedyah glared at her, as if to reprimand her for speaking directly to the king, then focused on Lucjan again. "He hasn't seen us, he doesn't know that we know about him."

"Actually, that's wrong," Nadzia interrupted. She caught everyone's attention.

"Excuse me?"

"The mist was his way of knowing if anyone was trying to cross into his territory. By crossing the bridge, you actually trespassed." Nadzia liked the power she held with her knowledge of their world and what was going on in it. "He knows everything that happens in his land. He might not know who it was, but he knows that a group of people entered his territory, and it won't take a genius to figure out who they were or why they were there."

"That's what I was worried about," Lucjan said sternly, looking at Hedyah.

She quickly fell down to her knee, head low. "I disobeyed an order and I was out of line for thinking I was right."

"Get up," Lucjan ordered, embarrassed by his friend kneeling to him. "The damage is done."

Hedyah stood up again.

"This means that everything she said is true, doesn't it?" Dacey asked, finally. Nadzia wanted to scream with joy at the first sign of trust, or at least belief, she'd seen since she'd met them.

"Maybe not everything, but she does have valid information about Malkiya," Lucjan answered. He studied her in silence, and while everyone's eyes were on her no gaze felt as heavy as his.

"You will tell us everything you know, and you'll help us against Malkiya. You will be treated like a guest in return."

Nadzia bit her lip to repress her smile. "It'd be my pleasure."

"We're trusting her, now?" Hedyah asked, looking upset.

"We're only making a deal beneficial to both, it doesn't mean we trust her."

"Of course," Nadzia nodded. She didn't really care about having their unconditional trust. She just wanted to sleep in a real bed and have the freedom to work out how to get back to her own world.

"Please take her to her room," Lucjan said without addressing anyone. Xayvion stepped forward and gestured for Nadzia to follow him. She was a little disappointed that they were already dismissing her, but she had already achieved so much that day and didn't want to push her luck.

She walked beside Xayvion and frowned when she noticed how sure he looked of where he was headed.

"Wait, you already had a room ready for me?" His silence was answer enough. "Why did you make me spend all that time in a cold cell if you'd already decided to believe me?"

"Lucjan wanted proof before he decided. If Hedyah's story turned out to be different to yours, the room would just have been vacant, and you would have gone back to the cell." *Or would have been killed*, is what he didn't say.

"Way to overcomplicate things," she mumbled.

He opened the door to her room and she didn't wait a second before she ran in and jumped on the bed. *Softness*, she thought. *Real sheets*. She smiled into the pillow.

"You have your own room, but you're not allowed to go anywhere on your own," he announced. "You need to have one of us with you at all times."

Her head snapped up. "Aren't I supposed to be a guest?"

"We still haven't confirmed your identity and motives, so we still need to keep an eye on you. It's nothing personal," he tried to make up for it.

"It's purely personal," she whispered to herself.

"Another thing," he said. "You will have your meals with us."

Excitement shot through her body. She had always wanted to experience what meals with royals in a castle felt like. Despite the situation she was in, the idea still made her feel good.

She placed her chin on her hand. "I'll wait for you to come get me for dinner, then?" She teased, smiling.

He turned and left the room as if she hadn't said anything, which made her chuckle. He didn't give away any sign, but she knew him better than anyone and she knew he was a little flustered.

She put her head back on the pillow and closed her eyes. She let herself smile.

Maybe things were taking a turn for the better.

NAME: Xayvion

HEIGHT: 179 cm / 5'10"

AGE: 24

HAIR COLOR: black

EYE COLOR: brown

ENTITY: empath,
born human

5.

Nadzia had barely slept in days and the bed was so soft and comfortable that it only took her a moment to fall asleep. She wasn't planning on sleeping at all, actually. She really wanted to explore the bedroom and think about the meaning of life just like she had during her lonely time in the cell, but exhaustion hit and ruined her plans.

There was a knock at the door and Nadzia awoke with a start. She quickly wiped the drool off her chin and glanced at the window. It was dark outside. The person knocked a second time, and she finally stumbled off the bed and opened the door just enough to show half of her face.

"Yes?"

Xayvion raised an eyebrow at her in question. "We're expected for dinner."

"Oh, right," she said. "Give me a minute."

She closed the door in his face before he had the time to reply. Quickly scanning the room, she ran to the door on the other side of it. She heaved a sigh of relief when she realized that it was, indeed, a bathroom. Sure, it wasn't the modern bathroom she was used to, but it was way more civilized than the disgusting prison toilet.

She definitely needed a bath. And to change her clothes. But they were probably already late and if she took too long she feared Xayvion would come to get her himself. Lucjan wouldn't be happy about the delay, either.

She shouldn't have fallen asleep.

Running back into her room, she opened the big wardrobe and was happy to see that it was full of clothes. She picked the first shirt, pair of pants and shoes she found and went back into the bathroom. Undressing quickly, she tried to wash as fast as she could, at least to make sure she didn't stink, then she put on her new clothes. She hated not having decent soap, or some deodorant. She found a ribbon and used it to tie her curly, unruly hair. She looked in the mirror and nodded. That was the best she could do for now.

When she walked out of her room, Xayvion looked at her with an irritated expression. "Took you long enough."

"Thanks for not barging in," she replied simply.

He examined her from head to toe as they headed to the dining hall.

"Those clothes suit you," he said.

"Were you tired of seeing me in my hoodie?" She joked.

"Hoodie?" He asked, confused.

Again, the fact that he had no idea what a hoodie was felt hilarious. She knew she was from a different world, and era, but moments like this were the only times she actually *felt* it. She explained to him that a hoodie was the piece of clothing she had been wearing earlier and he listened and nodded, looking genuinely interested.

The dining hall was almost as big as a football field— 70 meters long if she remembered correctly from her manuscript. Obviously it wasn't small, but Nadzia had thought it would be even bigger in real life, so she was a little disappointed. She made a mental note to make it even bigger once she went back.

There were three long tables which were mostly empty. The castle was big, but it didn't have enough people in it to fill the dining hall. There were only some guards that had just finished their shift, and King Lucjan sitting at the head of the table with his inner circle. Nadzia and Xayvion walked towards the head table and she tried not to focus on the fact that they were all watching her every move.

Lucjan glared at her when they arrived, probably because they were late and everyone had already started eating. Nadzia gave him an apologetic smile and sat in the empty seat next to Dacey. She was pleased to notice that he had changed his appearance slightly. His hair was red instead of blond and the birthmark was gone.

Xayvion took a seat at the other side of the table, beside Lucjan. To his left, there was Faleece and then Hedyah.

"I'm sorry," Nadzia apologized, "I fell asleep."

Lucjan did not to reply and just gestured for everyone to continue eating. A servant that seemed to appear out of nowhere put a plate with hot meat and bread in front of her. Nadzia stared at it in awe for a long while, her stomach letting out a loud growl. How she had missed meat... The hard bread and weird soup they had given her when she was in the cell had been a nightmare.

"Aren't you going to eat?" Dacey whispered to her.

"I haven't seen proper food in a while, leave me alone," she replied, getting defensive.

It didn't take long for her to pick up her cutlery and start eating after that. She was so satisfied after her first bite that she felt like laughing. She glanced up just for a second to find Xayvion looking away, holding back a smile.

They ate in silence for a while. Nadzia focused on the guards laughing and the scraping of knives against plates, trying to distract herself from the awkwardness..

At some point, Dacey half turned towards Nadzia. "What's your world like?"

She could tell he had been holding back from asking for a while. Hedyah sent him an icy glare but he ignored her.

"It's completely different to here, more modern," Nadzia started, thinking of how she could possibly explain it so they would understand.

"In what way?"

"Well, we're all human and don't have any kind of magic, but we've managed to build machines that do things for us. For example, we can have light inside our houses without using fire. We have a constant supply of water, both hot and cold, that comes out of faucets which we can open and close whenever we want. We can communicate with people from other parts of the world without having to send a physical message. We can travel in carriages that don't need horses to move and we can fly." She shrugged. "We adapted to make up for our shortcomings, I guess."

"That sounds like magic to me," Lucjan replied.

She smiled at that, pleased to realize he was interested in what she was saying. "It's all just science, but it does feel like magic sometimes."

Faleece tapped Xayvion's arm gently. He turned to look at her and she signed something to him. Nadzia was about to open her mouth to speak, but stopped herself. She knew what Faleece was saying because she had learned sign language before she'd started writing her novel, but maybe she could keep at least *one* secret. It might come in useful someday.

"Faleece would like to know why you wrote the story you claim we're in," he said.

"You have storytellers here in this world as well," Nadzia started. "Just like here, we write for fun and entertainment. Some people, like me, write about magic because the lack of it in our lives makes us feel like we're missing a piece, like we need something *more*."

Faleece nodded both to tell her she'd understood her point, and thank her for her reply. Then, she turned slightly towards Xayvion again. *'Can we really trust her?'* She signed. They were still for a few moments, warm brown eyes staring into grey ones, then he looked away. He was clever enough not to translate that and pretended she hadn't said anything.

The table fell silent again, tension that wasn't there before started making its way into the group. Nadzia tried to think of something she could do, or say, to kill the awkward atmosphere.

"Will I be allowed to attend your meetings?" She asked Lucjan.

"Only when we need you," he replied. "I hope you remember our deal. You need to tell us everything you know."

"Don't worry, I will."

"And if you end up being useless, we'll just get rid of you," Hedyah added, an evil grin on her face. To Nadzia's horror, Lucjan didn't disagree.

One way or another, Nadzia had to find a way of being useful to them constantly or she'd end up dead before she could go home.

She started to think about her house. It was a small apartment where she lived alone. It was messy and chaotic but it was home. She thought of Sanna, of how she'd left her that day. What was going on in her world now? Had she completely disappeared? Would her family file a missing person claim? Would she be considered dead? Would that petty argument be the last conversation she'd ever had with her best friend?

"Can I ask you a favor?" She asked, looking at Lucjan.

"You're in no position to be asking favors of the king," Hedyah replied.

"Shut up." It might have been the sadness and fear she was feeling at the moment, but for the first time Nadzia's tone was firm and serious. She felt Hedyah's eyes burning into her but she didn't even look in her direction.

"What favor?" Lucjan asked.

"I want you to help me find a way to go back home, to my world." She saw he was about to comment, so added, "I know you still don't believe my story, but it's a fact that I'm very far from home and that I want— no, I *need* to go back sooner or later. I have a family, and friends. I have no idea if they're waiting for me or not. I don't even know if time is passing normally in my world or if it has somehow stopped."

He seemed to consider it seriously, and Nadzia could see his brain working behind his dark eyes.

"Alright, we'll help," he said, "but don't count on us too much. There's no record of a situation like yours so we can't know for sure that we'll actually be able to find what you need."

"All I ask is that you at least try to help me," she replied quietly, "that's all."

He nodded in acknowledgment. Xayvion's gaze felt heavy on her and for once she wished he couldn't feel what she was feeling. For once, she wanted the privacy to be miserable alone.

After dinner when everyone had been dismissed, Xayvion walked her back to her room, through the cold, empty hallways that could definitely use a little more decor other than the occasional candles on the walls. Neither of them talked as they walked, and she made sure he didn't get the chance to do so once at her door either, by quickly slipping inside her room and shutting the door in his face.

She spent the next hour crying in the bathtub.

6.

The king and his inner circle were busy in a private meeting. Sightly upset she wasn't in there with them, Nadzia ended up wandering aimlessly around the palace. A guard followed her every movement, making her feel every bit the prisoner she still was.

Nadzia started on the second floor, passing by the meeting room a few more times than necessary in the hope she could eavesdrop what was being said. The fourth time around, the two guards stationed by the door and the one following her all cleared their throats to get her attention, then proceeded to glare at her and gestured for her to walk away. With an awkward smile she turned and did as she had been told.

Nadzia then proceeded to open all the doors she could find. If her guard didn't specifically tell her not to, then she was going to try and peak inside. She hadn't planned every single room in the castle in her story after all, so it was certainly going to be an adventure.

Nadzia found another meeting room, the larger one Lucjan used for official meetings. The walls were covered in paintings of legends and stories of old kings and queens. On the wall behind the bigger chair at the head of the table was the drawing of a figure, very clearly Lucjan, standing on a pile of deformed bodies, with a light shining from behind him. Nadzia rolled her eyes. She was sure he hadn't been the one to commission the drawing, but he clearly enjoyed the way people saw him.

The next door she opened took her into a living area with three couches, a fireplace and a pool table. It was a small, cozy space. When writing her book, she'd never given her characters the time to relax or do mundane things. She took a moment to imagine what that room would be like with them in it. She imagined Hedyah and Faleece cuddling openly in front of the fire. She imagined Xayvion trying to teach Dacey how to play pool, and the clumsy blond failing miserably at every attempt. She imagined Lucjan in a corner by himself reading a book. She couldn't help a fond smile from forming on her lips. She saw the weird look the guard gave her, as if she were crazy, and raised an eyebrow at him challenging him to comment. He didn't take the bait.

Back in the corridor again, she closed the door and walked to the next one, letting out a sigh of relief at the sight of books.

"Make yourself comfortable," she told the guard. "We're going to be here for a while."

Nadzia walked over to the shelves and carefully read the labels and titles, hopefully looking for something that sounded familiar or that could possibly have something to do with traveling. With a grin on her face, she gestured for the guard to follow her. She piled books into his arms, ordering him to take them to a table and return for more. He obeyed without complaint which made Nadzia feel she had a little bit of control over her life again.

After she'd hoarded a fair number of books, she wandered over to the table and started checking them out in detail. Unfortunately, this process was faster than she had thought it would be as she quickly passed from one book to another given nothing she read was close to what she needed. She kept searching nonetheless.

Time passed and she heard her guard mumbling complaints to himself, although he never said anything to her directly, so she kept reading. Lunchtime passed and the light coming through the window slowly became less and less bright.

Nadzia kept walking back and forth from the shelves to the table with books, startling her sleepy guard awake every time she groaned in frustration or dropped a book.

"Such a big place and not a single useful book," she complained. She eyed the guard suspiciously. "Can I get into the secret part?"

His eyes widened and Nadzia felt the need to roll hers. She wondered why they had forced such a clumsy, naive individual to be her guard for the day. She felt slightly bad for him.

"What secret part?" He asked, pretending to not know what she was talking about.

Nadzia remembered how to get in, but she couldn't do it without official permission, and trying to sneak in when she was being watched wasn't a wise idea.

"The secret library," she explained. "Am I allowed to go in? You're with me after all."

"I'm afraid I don't know what you're talking about," he replied quickly.

She groaned in frustration once more, then nodded in defeat.

Nadzia made a mental note to ask Lucjan for permission. After all, he *had* said he would try to help her so it ought to be okay for her to ask. She stopped to think about it for a moment, then shook her head. It hadn't been long since she'd unloaded an enormous amount of information on him and made him aware she knew more than she should. He didn't trust her so if she went to him now and demanded to see something that wasn't supposed to be open to the public, it probably wouldn't end well. Maybe she should wait a few days before asking, to get him used to her presence and requests.

Momentarily putting an end to her fruitless research, she replaced the remaining books and finally left the library to continue the tour of the castle she had started that morning.

Nadzia followed the sound of people fighting and stopped in front of the door of one of the training rooms. She realized it was the valkyries' training room when she noticed all the people in there were women.

Towards her right, at the end of the room and far from everyone else, Hedyah and Faleece were parrying with each other. They had clearly been doing it for a while, but the sweat on their skin was the only sign of it. They didn't seem worn out at all.

The two of them took on a high guard, Faleece's mouth stretching into a smirk. Hedyah grinned back and attacked.

Faleece blocked her, faked an attack then retreated. From the way they moved it was clear they weren't really fighting, but playing, although there was still some seriousness to it. Faleece's black hair flew around as she gracefully fought with Hedyah. Nadzia was surprised to hear Hedyah let out a laugh.

Nadzia watched them with a small smile on her face. They looked like each other's opposites, and yet they also looked as if they were made for each other, and each other only. Where Hedyah was light, curvy, and tall, Faleece was dark, thin and just a little bit shorter than her girlfriend. While Faleece couldn't physically talk, Hedyah sometimes talked more than she should, and with great confidence. Hedyah was the reckless one, while Faleece had to calm her down or get her out of trouble. They completed each other.

Seeing them together, happy and carefree, made Nadzia's heart lighter. She might be going through a crisis in her life, but at least she had had the chance to experience all this in person. It was way more than any other writer could claim to have done.

NAME: Lucjan
HEIGHT: 185 cm / 6'1"
AGE: 300+
HAIR COLOR: brown
EYE COLOR: dark brown
ENTITY: former deity

7.

She was jolted awake. Again.

The loud noises came from outside. Nadzia sat up quickly and opened the windows to see what all the commotion was about.

Soldiers were rushing into the castle courtyard on their horses. They were talking over one another and their faces were troubled. Even the horses seemed unable to withstand all the noise, protesting loudly in return. Along with them, a few injured men were being dragged inside the castle.

Nadzia threw on some clothes as quickly as she could, then rushed towards the door of her room. When she opened it, she found Xayvion standing there, his hand up ready to knock.

"Something's happened, you need to be there, too," he said.

She nodded and followed him to the meeting room, where Lucjan and Dacey were already waiting for them.

"What's going on?"

"When I sent Hedyah to check what was going on after the attacks started, I had also sent soldiers to guard the villages near Lake Naraka," Lucjan said. "At first, the beasts seemed to stay away from the villages that were protected, but have now attacked. The village they attacked was way closer to us than the others, which isn't a good sign."

"He's testing his beasts to see how close he can get to you," Nadzia continued for him.

Lucjan nodded, troubled.

"We don't know much more about the situation," Dacey explained. "Hedyah and Faleece are currently with the soldiers. Some are injured but we're waiting to hear back from them."

"Does this happen in your book?" Lucjan asked, and that's when Nadzia knew he was getting desperate. He didn't know how to keep his composure when Malkiya was involved. "Did you plan this, too?"

She felt bad for him. For all the things she'd made him go through just for the sake of it.

She shook her head. "I hadn't written about this specific attack, something doesn't add up."

"If the bullshit you've told us over the past days is true, then all of this is your fault. You created us, you made Malkiya choose that path, made him come back," he accused Nadzia, angrily. Clearly, he had given her story some thought. Dacey and Xayvion watched as Lucjan stepped forwards at every word, closer to her, until he was inches from her. His six foot one frame was towering over Nadzia's five foot five. "*You* made him attack the villages. *You* made him kill people."

It took her a second to find her voice again, and when she spoke it was weak and shaky. "None of this was ever supposed to be real."

"But it is," he hissed.

The eyes that looked into hers were so sad, desperate and angry. But Nadzia didn't feel scared. She felt guilty.

"For what it's worth, I'm really sorry," she confessed, sincerely. "I'm sorry for making you suffer all those years, and I'm sorry for getting you banned from the upper realms. I'm sorry for creating Malkiya the way he is and for making the people you promised to keep safe suffer."

Xayvion stepped forward and gently put his hand on Lucjan's arm, silently telling him to calm down. Lucjan seemed to get the message and stepped back, although his expression didn't change. If he hadn't trusted her before, Nadzia was sure that now he wanted nothing more than for her to feel miserable, preferably out of sight.

The doors opened and Hedyah and Faleece walked in. There were bloodstains on their clothes from helping the injured soldiers into the castle.

"Tell me you've something relevant to report," Lucjan said harshly. He looked tired.

They both nodded and he gestured for them to speak.

"There was only one beast that attacked. It didn't attack the village but focused on the soldiers," Hedyah started. "They said it looked like a huge black wolf. From the bites and cuts on the injured, both its teeth and claws seem bigger than any canine's I've ever seen."

Nadzia's eyes widened in realization.

"The hell hound," she whispered to herself.

Unfortunately for her, Lucjan heard, and was anything but happy to see her reaction.

"What?"

"It's a hell hound, he's Malkiya's pet and most loyal servant." She frowned, confused and worried. "But he's not supposed to be here yet, it's too early. Malkiya was supposed to summon him from the underworld way later in the story. This doesn't make sense."

"None of this makes fucking sense," Lucjan snapped.

She looked away in shame.

"How come the plot is changing? This is your book, isn't it?" Hedyah said accusingly. She was as angry as Lucjan. "It should follow what you wrote."

Nadzia actually stopped to think about it. She felt stupid for not realizing soon what was going on.

"I didn't come here in someone else's body. I am literally a new character that has appeared in the story. As if that weren't enough to throw things off balance, my story got tangled up with yours, the main characters," she slowly explained. "The plot had already changed, I just didn't realize it."

Lucjan ran a hand through his hair, looking as if he wanted to rip it out. Dacey was the only one in the room, apart from Nadzia, who couldn't stop noticing how it seemed as if he was about to lose control. Xayvion, Hedyah and Faleece, however, didn't seem concerned about his behavior.

He wasn't supposed to be like this. King Lucjan was wise, calm and collected. He was older than anyone could guess and had had experience both in war and life. Even if he were one of the youngest and most recent war gods, he was still more mature than anyone else currently alive in his kingdom, as he was a few centuries their senior.

Only one person could make him turn into such a mess, and that was Malkiya. The friend who fought by his side for centuries. The friend who was banished for experimenting with magic darker than anyone could imagine. The friend he thought had died years before. The friend he hoped had died, because his being alive would only have meant hell.

But alive he was, and hell was what he was causing.

Lucjan had no intention of letting Nadzia off so easily.

"You're going to tell me everything you know, now," he demanded.

Despite knowing it was dangerous for her to say it, she had to warn him anyway. "If the story is changing, I can't promise that what I tell you will be accurate."

He rolled his eyes in frustration. "I don't care, anything that could be remotely true would be useful at this stage. We need to know what we're up against."

She waited a moment, debating whether she should leave some details out or not. She shook her head. It was better to tell him the whole story from the beginning. It would hurt, but he needed to know.

"When you two were banished from the upper realms and literally thrown into the mortal world, they made sure to send you to two different locations. I know you tried to find Malkiya again, thinking you could help each other out to start again here in this world. You didn't find him, not because you didn't look closely or attentively enough, but because he didn't want to be found. He hid purposely from you." Lucjan's eyes showed hurt, but he didn't seem surprised. "He watched you from afar and waited for you to give up before permanently occupying Mount Elysium. He fought with the creatures living in the mountains and claimed a place for himself that was far away and secluded. He studied dark magic day and night and practiced on everything and everyone he could get his hands on. With much trial and error, he managed to achieve a satisfactory result, which is why it took him so many years to start his attacks on the villages."

She sighed. Her next words wouldn't be enough to make up for all the information she had just dumped on him, but she hoped it would still feel like something they could use to their advantage. "His experiments drove him mad, but they also made him more vulnerable."

"What exactly are these experiments you're talking about? What has he created?"

"He went to the underworld and looked for souls with the most resentful anger he could find, offering them deals to bring them back to this world, as living dead. All they want to do is kill, and he offered them the opportunity to do so."

"They're like ghosts, then?" Dacey asked, a little confused.

"Not at all, they're very much corporeal."

He didn't look happy with her answer.

Xayvion must have felt her hesitating, so he asked, "there's something else, isn't there?"

She nodded. "He also brought back demons, creatures of any kind and form he could find. Some look like reptiles, others are canines, others are mixes of several beasts. In this case too, they are here to kill."

"All these creatures and demons... are they already in this world?"

"Initially I would have said no, but seeing how fast things are moving and the fact that Cael, his hell hound, is already here, I'm afraid he's very close to reaching the number of recruits he needs. Which explains his recents attacks on both the villages and your soldiers."

"So what you're saying is that the war you predicted will happen sooner rather than later," Lucjan finished.

"Yes."

"But we can do this, can't we?" Dacey asked, hopefully. "We all have experience in battle, and magic wielders in our army."

"You can't beat demon beasts with simple swords and a little magic," Nadzia said, and she had to admit she felt a little bad for replying in *that* tone. But in all honesty, she was silently freaking out. *She* didn't have experience in battle, she'd never even held a sword or a dagger. *She* didn't have magic and she *surely* couldn't survive an encounter with a demon, or even a normal animal. Dacey dismissing the problem in that way felt like a personal insult to her.

"What do you suggest we do?" The king asked, seriously curious to know.

She tilted her head at him, asking an obvious question. "Do you know who has access to both magic and magical beasts?"

A cold silence fell and Nadzia had to hold back a hysterical laugh. It wasn't the time to lose her mind. Yet.

"Elves," she said finally, since no one seemed intent on saying it out loud.

In her original plot, the elves were only briefly mentioned. They weren't part of the story. But everything had changed now and they wouldn't have time to train the soldiers properly. They needed more people and they needed more power.

Hedyah scoffed. "We have a treaty with them, and we let them live on our land, but that doesn't mean they'll help us. It's no secret that they hate us."

"King Eryx will never agree to help us," Lucjan admitted, bitterly.

"Well, luckily for you Eryx is no longer king," Nadzia said cheerfully. "He died a couple years ago and now his son Kagen is king."

He didn't seem to trust her information. "We haven't heard about any of this."

"Of course you haven't, you know what elves are like. They still don't trust you despite the treaty, and always try to make sure information doesn't leak outside their territory."

"You think he's going to be different to his father?"

It was common knowledge that King Eryx had been old, cruel and proud. Kagen, however, was different. Even if he hadn't appeared in her original plot, Kagen was still a character she herself had created. She'd just never ended up using him in the story. There was a possibility he would actually exist in this world and be just like Nadzia had imagined him.

"He might not agree right away, but I'm confident we can convince him," she said. Faking confidence had become strangely easy for her. None of them noticed that she was *praying* that what she'd just said was true.

"If we *do* manage to get them on our side and have magical beasts fighting alongside us, how will our soldiers fight if their swords aren't enough to kill the demons?" Dacey asked.

Lucjan answered before Nadzia could. "Demons have an aversion to gold. If we melt iron with gold to make new weapons, that should be enough to kill them."

"Where do we find enough gold to make swords for our entire army?" Hedyah asked.

Nadzia could see Lucjan was thinking hard.

"I don't have much, but there's some gold in the royal collection from previous kings and queens. We can use that to start the process."

"I heard our coast used to be famous for gold," Xayvion added, earning a nod from Lucjan.

"We should go to the coast to retrieve the gold we need and, in the meantime, we need to hire all the blacksmiths of the town and nearby villages to work as fast as they can on the new weapons. We *have* to be ready." Before anyone could ask any questions, he added. "I'll go to the coast. Hedyah you come with me. Xayvion, Dacey and Faleece will go to the Elf Realm to ask their king for assistance." Then, he turned to Nadzia. "*You* will go with them. Everything is riding on your shoulders, so you'd better succeed."

She couldn't refuse, so just nodded. She'd put herself in this situation and had to see it through.

"We all set off tomorrow at dawn. It'll take the rest of the day to make all the necessary arrangements."

Nadzia looked around at the others and noticed how everyone was suddenly standing straighter, more confidently. It was almost as if the prospect of war made them feel more alive, and that thought scared her.

8.

No one slept well that night, there was too much to prepare. They had to contact all the blacksmiths in town, and if they weren't enough, the ones in the nearby villages as well. They needed instructing as to how the weapons should be made and understand they didn't have enough time to take things slowly. They had to prepare the carriages that would go back and forth to bring the gold back to the city, and needed to pack food and clothes for themselves.

A little before dawn, everyone grouped together in front of the castle, ready to go.

Lucjan mounted his horse and turned to Nadzia's group.

"You need to convince the new elf king to ally with us. Get his support, whatever it takes." His eyes rested on Xayvion, his expression becoming even more serious, "You know what to do."

It felt like a secret code and a warning.

Lucjan didn't waste time on motivational speeches and set off immediately. Hedyah looked back at Faleece once before she followed him. Her expression was neutral, but there was a hint of worry in her eyes, as if she were scared about not having Faleece with her so she could make sure she was safe at all times.

Xayvion approached Nadzia. "Can you ride a horse?"

Nadzia froze remembering she couldn't, in fact, ride a horse. Never in her life had she been given the chance to try. Her panicky expression was enough of an answer for him.

"Here, let me help," he said.

He showed her where to put her foot to mount the horse— she gasped at how high up she was— then he showed her how to hold the reins and move with the horse. It was a brief explanation, but helpful enough for her to mount her horse and sit on it when they started moving off.

Xayvion rode next to Nadzia to guide her and make sure she didn't do anything that would scare the horse and make her fall.

The feeling of the horse under her made Nadzia uncomfortable. It was a weird feeling knowing she was on an animal's back. She was worried she would hurt it with her weight. She tried to focus on the journey and city around her to distract herself from the animal and how her body didn't seem to adjust to the way they were moving. The streets were busy, stands with products on display were set up in front of shops, owners cheerfully invited people to come closer and take a look at what they were selling and the quality of their products. Nadzia saw a woman sweeping the entrance to a pub and children playing with a ball. She was surprised to see so much hustle and bustle so early on in the day, but Xayvion soon sated her curiosity by telling her that everyone there started their days early. This wasn't a detail she had specified when she wrote the novel, so she didn't know. Nadzia felt a little embarrassed he had had to explain it.

As soon as they managed to leave the center of the city their pace quickened. From then on the houses were more spaced out and the scenery full of farms and fields. Many of the men and women from the city, the ones that didn't have shops or taverns of their own, were employed working in these fields.

"How are you doing?" Xayvion asked after a while.

She didn't want to sound vulgar by telling him exactly *what* part of her body was hurting, nor did she wish to complain so soon into their journey, choosing to give him a tight lipped smile instead. "All good."

"First time riding a horse, huh?" Dacey said, riding closer to the two of them.

"Yep." She had a feeling that if she started talking they'd eventually hear the strain in her voice and understand that her body was hurting and she didn't want them to see how weak she really was compared to them.

Oh, how she missed cars…

"Do you have horses in your world?" He asked.

"Yes, but we don't really use them to travel around like this anymore," she replied.

"You know, I was wondering," he started, and Nadzia saw Xayvion shake his head as if to say '*Here we go again*'. "What do armies use to fight in your world?"

That was random. Nadzia looked at Xayvion, eyes wide, but he just shrugged.

"Well, we have weapons, but as I explained the other day, they're machines we invented. They do the job for us most of the time and cause way more damage than a simple sword. Our weapons are usually for fighting at a distance, like you'd do with a bow and arrow I guess." It felt weird to try and explain her world to them, and even weirder that she didn't exactly know how to do so. It felt a lot like those situations in which someone asks you to explain the meaning of a word, and you end up explaining it simply by repeating the word.

But apparently it was enough for Dacey to create an image in his head and he nodded, his mouth forming an 'O', his eyes clearly not focused on the reality in front of him. He fell quiet for a long while after that and Nadzia imagined he was making up his own version of her world in his mind.

Nadzia took advantage of the silence— and the long way they still had to go— to lose herself in her thoughts as well.

It had been a week since she'd appeared in her book, and surprisingly it didn't actually feel that long. The odd situation she was in with her characters had made her temporarily forget that she needed to get home. Even though she had returned to her senses long enough to ask them to help her do so, and to start looking for clues herself, Nadzia knew it wasn't going to happen any time soon. They had a lot to take care of first, and even she couldn't afford to focus on anything else. Nadzia was inside her book and if the war did happen soon, she was going to be in a lot of danger. She needed to come up with a plan to protect herself, before she could even think about how to get home.

She glanced at her three companions, all of them silent and focused on the road ahead. She had created them, and yet, they weren't like she had made them at all. In her original plot Faleece had been way more of an extrovert. There was hardly any part of the real Faleece that reminded her of the person she'd written about. Dacey was more talkative and childlike than she'd planned. Lucjan was supposed to be way more friendly and kind, but it made sense that he wasn't like that at present considering Nadzia had just turned his world upside down. Xayvion and Hedyah seemed to be the only ones that somehow felt close to their original characters. She was curious to see what the remaining characters were like.

She was especially curious about Kagen. When she'd first written the outline to her novel she'd planned his name and a few traits of his personality, nothing more. When she got to writing the story, she realized that the elves didn't fit in as well as she'd hoped, so ended up just mentioning them briefly. The Elf Realm was only partially written. What should she expect from them? Would Kagen be like the character she had chosen initially, or would he have created a new personality for himself? To be honest, Nadzia didn't even know what kind of magical creatures they would end up seeing there. She had sketched some at the time, but had no idea if any of them would be in the story or if she would find new ones she hadn't even thought of. Going to the Elf Realm was both exciting and scary.

After a while they stopped to let the horses drink and Nadzia almost had to throw herself off her horse to dismount. After hours of riding she couldn't feel her legs, her butt felt numb and her back was aching. She regretted not being more athletic. If only she had done some kind of exercise, ever, during the course of her life, she would at least have some muscles to help her ride.

"How long till we get there?" She asked, the pain evident in her voice.

"There's still a long way to go," Xayvion replied, giving her a small smile of encouragement.

Xayvion looked fine and energetic. He was perfectly comfortable riding and the journey hadn't tired him at all. Despite the sun beating down on them, there wasn't a single drop of sweat on his golden brown skin. The sight of him still looking perfect and handsome like that compared to what she thought she looked like at that moment made her grimace.

She had no idea how long she could keep going before her body started to literally fall apart, but didn't have any other choice, so they all mounted their horses again and continued on their journey until past dark. Nadia figured it was close to midnight when her companions finally chose a spot to rest.

They lit a fire to cook themselves some food and went to sleep, just laying down on the grass. It felt weird and uncomfortable for Nadzia to sleep on the ground. She always slept on beds, never on hard surfaces like floors— the only exception was the poor excuse of a bed that was in the castle prison, but again, she hadn't really slept during those nights. What made everything more uncomfortable was the grass pricking her skin. Even using a jacket as a pillow didn't make it better.

She also didn't feel safe. Sleeping out in the open, in the middle of nowhere, made her think of horror movies she had seen and it unsettled her. Who knew what could happen? Maybe her own companions would be the ones to hurt her. They said they didn't trust her properly yet, even if they'd decided to let her work with them. Although they acted casually and in a friendly way with her now, she couldn't help but worry. The thought kept bugging her. It was one of the reasons why she had tried to lay down as far away as she could from the three of them, while still trying to be close enough to the fire not to die from cold.

She sighed and sat up, staring at the crackling fire.

"Can't sleep?"

She jumped at the voice. Lost in her own thoughts, she hadn't noticed that Xayvion had turned around and was looking at her.

She nodded. "Too many thoughts," she explained.

He stood up and went to sit next to her, smiling softly.

"Worried about the mission?" He asked.

"Worried about you guys, actually," she corrected him.

He frowned in confusion. "What do you mean?"

"Well, I know I've explained myself and my story to you many times already, but I also know not a single one of you actually believes or trusts me. Dacey is the only one who seems interested in knowing about my world, but it's for his own enjoyment, not because he really wants to know me," she explained. "I seriously don't know what to do to get you to trust me, and the more I try the more some of you seem to hate me. It's so frustrating, because I'd hoped we could be friends. I still hope we can be." She sighed. "But to be honest, I can't blame you for not liking me. I can't blame Lucjan for being furious with me, either. I'm the one who created this mess and made everyone suffer after all, so I deserve it."

"He's just upset because everything is happening so quickly," Xayvion replied, softly. "He's not one to hold grudges. And everyone makes mistakes, after all."

"Thank you for trying to cheer me up," she started, "but we both know you're lying."

They stared into each other's eyes silently for a while and Nadzia wished she could get a look inside his head to find out what he was thinking. But of one thing she could be sure: he was reading her emotions. She wondered what he was feeling from her because, frankly, she couldn't tell either. Both her head and her heart were a mess.

"Lucjan can be kind and forgiving," he said, eventually. His voice was low, soft and calming. A single word spoken by him felt like listening to a symphony. Like lying in a flower field on a warm day. She found it marvelous.

"Tell me about your friendship," she prompted.

"You wrote the story, you should know better than anyone else."

Her voice was quiet and vulnerable when she said, "I would like to hear it from you."

There was a flash of confusion in his eyes for a second, and he quickly looked away as if ashamed of something.

He nodded, cleared his voice, and started talking, looking straight into the fire. "Lucjan was banished from the upper realms a little more than ten years ago. When he arrived in Phexion, the city was a mess. The last king had recently died and there was no heir or anyone who could replace him. The council kept meeting to try and find a solution but they disregarded each other's ideas and opinions. With the lack of any kind of government, bandits started attacking the villages, and people from confining countries started attacking us. The elves, too, took that as an opportunity to fight us in order to try and break free from our treaty to get more privileges. There was no doubt that Lucjan was a supreme being. Even as a fallen god he was still more powerful than anyone in the kingdom. He took control and led the army to push enemies back at the borders, and punished the bandits. The elves were the hardest to deal with but Lucjan still managed to put King Eryx back in his place."

He stopped for a second to glance at Nadzia, looking genuinely surprised to see her interested in what he was saying. His expression darkened a little as he continued.

"When the bandits' attacks started, they went to my village, too. I wasn't there that day because my mother had sent me to Phexion to do some chores. When I returned, the whole village had been destroyed and there were no survivors." He stared into the fire, his eyes clouded by sadness. She gently pressed her leg against his for some wordless comfort. "I went back to the city to enlist, but was only thirteen at the time and Lucjan didn't want child soldiers. I kept insisting and even though he never let me fight with them, once he'd brought peace to the kingdom and returned to Phexion, he did allow me to start training. The council agreed to him taking over the position of king permanently and he took me under his wing. I grew up thinking of him as my older brother." He frowned, and added, "*that*, specifically, feels a little weird these days because he used to look much older than me but now it's hard to tell who has been around longer."

She chuckled at that.

"How old is he precisely?" She had never mentioned a specific number of years in the book and wondered whether Lucjan had ever told him.

"Over 300, I think," he replied, a weird expression on his face. "It sounds so strange to say that."

Nadzia nodded in agreement.

"I can see he thinks of you as a brother, too," she said eventually.

"He trusts me with the kingdom and that means so much to me."

There was silence for a while, and Nadzia could almost see his thoughts. She knew he was thinking back to his favorite and fondest memories with Lucjan. She wanted to ask him about those too, but had the feeling that it would be like intruding in his head and she didn't want to do that. She didn't want him to share something that personal, just for her to accidentally taint those memories and ruin them for him.

"You grew up with the others, right? Hedyah, Faleece and Dacey," she said, hoping he'd keep talking. She loved listening to him.

"From the moment I arrived in Phexion, I saw Hedyah and Faleece a lot. They are one and two years older than me respectively, and kids tend to spend time with those around their age. The Valkyries had special training, but we shared a space and often found ourselves together," he explained. "Dacey came a little later and fitted in just fine."

There was a small smile on his face and she felt her chest warm. She could see how much he cared for his friends. They were his family.

Then, out of nowhere, she said, "I want you to teach me how to fight." He looked surprised, but before he could ask her why, she added, "If there's going to be a war, I need to be able to protect myself at least."

He thought about it for a second, then stood up. "Come on then."

She got up and followed him away from their two companions who were miraculously still asleep despite their chatter.

"I'll teach you how to protect yourself in close combat first, okay?"

She nodded, waiting for instructions.

"Imagine someone's trying to punch you, or wield a knife at you," he said, then made the gesture in slow motion. "You need to bring your arm up and hit here with as much strength as you can muster." He indicated a point more or less in the middle of his arm. "Hitting the nerves here will automatically make the aggressor stop for a second and drop whatever they're holding. Take that moment of surprise to bring your other hand behind their head and press this point." He put his hand on her neck, thumb near the ear, middle finger pressing near the bone at the back. "While you do that, turn your other hand around to grab their wrist, then move and turn to throw the person on the floor. It's easier than it sounds, and most of the time they'll unconsciously help you throw them, mostly because of the grip you have on the back of their neck."

She nodded, soaking up every detail.

"Let's try it out, okay?" He asked. "Pretend to punch me and I'll defend myself."

She swung her fist at him and a moment later found herself on the ground, her arm stinging and the right side of her body aching from her sudden contact with the ground. If he hadn't explained every move to her beforehand, she wouldn't have known what had just taken place. It happened so fast that her brain didn't even have time to register the movements.

He helped her up and let her try. It took her a few gos before she actually managed to throw him, because at first

91

she was scared of using force, or accidentally touching the wrong part of his body and seriously hurting him. When she finally completed the move well she had to hold herself back from screaming happily. Xayvion laughed at her, holding a finger to his lips to remind her to keep quiet so they wouldn't wake the others.

They kept it up for another hour, and when they stopped and finally lay down to rest, Nadzia's arm and side ached, but she felt satisfied. Thankfully, she was exhausted enough to be able to fall asleep this time.

9.

The group resumed their journey a little too early for Nadzia's liking. She hadn't slept enough, her whole body felt heavier and ached even more than when she'd gone to sleep. She realized that maybe training with Xayvion the night before hadn't been such a smart idea.

Dacey seemed awfully cheerful that day and rode next to Nadzia. Xayvion took it as an excuse to flee and keep Faleece company, who was gracefully riding her horse ahead of them. From the look on her face, she seemed to enjoy the warmth of the sun on her rich brown skin.

"I tried shape-shifting into a horse once," Dacey explained, calling Nadzia's attention to him. "I wasn't really trying to, it just happened, and it freaked me out so much that I couldn't shift back. Someone took me for a real horse and thought I'd run away from my owner or something. They tried to catch me." He grimaced at the memory. "It was horrible."

"Did they try to ride you?" She asked. His rambling was actually nice to listen to.

"Oh my god, yes!" He said, dramatically. "It felt so weird."

She didn't know what to say to that. Instead, she ended up just looking at him. His features were relaxed and he looked younger than he was. How could he possibly be the same person she'd met that day in the pub? She was aware that people have layers and that they only share certain traits of their personality when they start to open up, but it still felt odd to witness such change in him. She had never written him as a cheerful character.

Nadzia hadn't realized she had been silently staring at him until he cleared his throat.

"Is everything alright?"

She looked away, embarrassed. "Yes, sorry. I was just thinking."

"Thinking about me?" He teased, smiling.

She nodded. "I was thinking about how different you are now compared to when we first met. It's like I've met two different people."

His expression became serious. "I didn't know who you were at first or if you were a threat to the kingdom or not, but now I can just be myself I guess."

His statement warmed Nadzia's heart. Maybe they were starting to trust her after all.

"I like this version of you way more than the first," she replied. "At least now you're not trying to knock me out."

"Sorry about that," he apologized quietly, an awkward smile on his face.

"It's alright, I understand your reasons."

It seemed as if he were holding himself back from saying something, looking at her then looking away, slightly opening his mouth then closing it the next second. After a while he said, "Why did my change surprise you? Aren't you the one that made me this way?"

He seemed interested in trying to understand her story and the fact that she'd created them. Nadzia found it cute.

"I've only been here in this world for a few days, but it is enough to make me realize that the story I created has a life of its own. The places expand even further than I designed them, and the people are way more complex than I'd planned. You're not just characters in a story, you're real people," she explained. "I'm ashamed to say I didn't expect that."

He nodded, processing what she'd just said.

"Why did you make me this way?"

She looked at him, confused by his question. "What do you mean?"

"Why did you give me this specific physical appearance? Why did you give me these powers? Things like that." He seemed cautious in asking.

"There wasn't a real reason if I have to be honest," she said. "I made a list of powers I wanted to include in my book at the beginning when I didn't even know what or how many characters I wanted. The creation of the characters happened later and it was kind of a random process I guess. I played around with character simulator sites and tried all the features until I found combinations that made me think 'Yes, that's them!'. Then I just paired the characters I created to the names and powers that seemed to fit them based on their appearance and personal stories."

"Character simulator sites?"

Once again Nadzia realized she was talking about something he had no idea even existed. It threw her every time.

"It's like… I'm not sure if it makes sense, but you have every feature in separate drawings. Like, you have separate drawings with different hairstyles, eyes, or body shapes, and then you put them together to create something that resembles a complete person."

He frowned in confusion but said, "I think I get it. Kind of."

She sighed, relieved. Technological things were more complicated to explain to someone who didn't even know what electricity was.

Faleece and Xayvion, who were riding in front of them, stopped near a pond to rest for a while. Dacey and Nadzia stopped next to them and dismounted.

Xayvion approached her as her feet touched the ground. "I was thinking of teaching you something else while we rest."

"My body is already full of bruises," she replied, her face silently asking for mercy.

He chuckled. "Don't worry, it's nothing that involves combat."

Nadzia couldn't deny that that caught her attention. "What do you want to teach me?"

"I was thinking about what you were saying last night, about needing to be able to protect yourself during the war. I don't think teaching you how to wield a sword would be a good idea. You wouldn't have enough time to be good enough to take care of yourself in the field. But you could potentially fight from afar, with bow and arrows."

She felt touched that he had been, sincerely, thinking of how to help her.

"I'd love to learn that," she replied.

"Well, I'll get Faleece to help you with it. I'm good with a bow, but she's better so it's best to leave it to her."

He left to talk to Faleece and Nadzia saw her turn to glance at her with a worried look on her face. Nadzia looked away, not wanting to see what she would say in response. Faleece was strangely hostile towards her in a passive way. She had expected Hedyah to not like her, and be open about it, but hadn't expected a similar reaction from Faleece.

Nadzia heard Xayvion call out to her and turned to see him gesturing for her to go over to them. Faleece was already holding a bow and some arrows.

"I'll be translating what she says, alright?" He announced.

Nadzia was lost for a second, then remembered that they didn't know she could understand sign language. She recomposed herself and nodded to him. Faleece passed her the bow.

As soon as Nadzia took the bow, Faleece started signing the explanation.

"Stand upright, feet at 90 degrees from your target," Xayvion translated.

Nadzia picked the tree in front of her as her target. She extended her arms and tried to pretend to shoot, but Faleece was quick to smack her hand.

Ouch.

"Keep a relaxed grip on the bow," Xayvion explained, holding back a chuckle.

Dacey sat on the ground next to them, enjoying the show.

Faleece passed Nadzia an arrow, showing her where she was supposed to place it, then where to put her fingers. Nadzia drew the bow.

"Pull the string backward using the muscles of your back rather than your arm," Faleece and Xayvion corrected her. "Pull back the string so that the index finger of the hand you're pulling with is under your chin, and the string touches your nose and lips."

Faleece adjusted her position a little, since Nadzia had accidentally forgotten some instructions as she tried to keep up with the new ones.

"Using your dominant eye, look down the arrow and align it with the target."

Nadzia did as she was told.

"Release."

She released the arrow. Everyone held their breaths, the only sound being the whistle of the arrow as it flew and hit the exact spot in the middle of the tree trunk she had pointed at. Everything seemed to halt and go silent for a few seconds in surprise. Nadzia couldn't believe it either. Knowing herself, she had not expected the arrow to go anywhere near the tree. *Beginner's luck.*

'*You're a natural,*' Faleece signed, smiling.

"Thank you," she replied, genuinely happy to have succeeded.

Distracted by her unexpected success, Nadzia hadn't realized she'd replied before Xayvion had had time to translate what Faleece had said.

"You understood her?" Xayvion asked. His tone sent shivers down her spine. Not a good sign.

She looked around at their surprised faces. "I imagined she complimented me?" But she already knew she was grasping at straws and that no one believed her.

"You can understand sign language, can't you?" Xayvion wasn't impressed by her effortless excuse.

"Yes, I can," she replied, giving in.

"Why didn't you just tell us?" Dacey asked. There was a little hurt in his voice and Nadzia noticed a hint of distrust in Xayvion's and Faleece's eyes, too. Did it really take so little to go back on all the progress she'd made so far?

"You didn't fully trust me and I wanted to keep at least one secret to myself," she admitted. "As far as I know, you could have used sign language to plan my execution, for example."

From their faces she could see they understood why she'd kept it secret, but that didn't make them less worried. They looked at her as if she were a stranger and she hated that.

She scoffed. "Really, now? That was enough for you to start considering me as your enemy again? That's ridiculous." They didn't reply and she shook her head in disbelief. She looked at Xayvion hoping to see him give in, but his expression was hard. Her voice was almost a whisper when she said, "I thought we were making progress. I thought we were becoming friends."

Feeling hurt she turned and walked back to her horse. She mounted it and waited for them to do the same. They resumed their journey in silence. Nadzia tried to keep herself separate from them, and they didn't seem to mind the distance, nor the silence.

Nadzia was angry at herself for accidentally exposing the only thing she'd promised herself to keep secret. She was especially angry at and disappointed with them, for having their trust broken so easily. They had been casual with her, treating her well, taking care of her and worrying about her. They'd started acting more like themselves and opening up.

They'd been showing genuine interest in her and the way she lived in her world. Nadzia had taken it as a sign that they were getting closer, that they were beginning to believe her. But if it was so easy to go back to square one, then the truth was that they had never trusted her to begin with. They'd only let their guard down around her because they felt comfortable. She realized that they'd probably never even meant to get close to her. It had just happened.

They passed the village where she'd first met Dacey, and then the fields in which she'd appeared a little over a week before.

That night Nadzia couldn't sleep, feeling even more unsafe than the night before now she had renewed their feeling of distrust for her. She spent the night staring at the stars and wishing she could just go home, right there and then.

They travelled for another half day before finally arriving at the forest surrounding the Elf Realm. Entering without the elves' permission was considered an act of war, so they stopped and waited a few feet from the first line of trees.

It didn't take long for two elf soldiers to come out of the forest.

"What is your business here?"

Xayvion straightened himself.

"In the name of King Lucjan, we're here to ask permission to see King Kagen."

10.

The horses were left outside the forest, tied to the trees to make sure they didn't wander off. The group followed the two elf soldiers along a path into their realm.

It had all happened too easily. People from a kingdom they were at peace with but still considered enemies had come to the elves' door and they'd just let them in, without asking why. They didn't show signs of not being okay with them being there, either. Nadzia knew she couldn't be the only one unsettled by what was happening.

She distracted herself from her anxious thoughts by looking around. After the first few meters which were dense with trees, the flat terrain turned into hills and then mountains. In amongst the trees, Nadzia sometimes glimpsed cottages and doors on hillsides. She had always liked the idea of houses inside hills, and was satisfied that her idea had come to life without her actually writing about it.

The elf palace was built into the side of the mountain and its huge entrance looked like a temple. It expanded into the entire mountain and then some, spreading with hallways and rooms underground as well.

The guards stationed outside the entrance were the only other sign of life the group had seen since entering the elves' territory. They barely even looked at the group as they passed and walked inside.

Nadzia and the others walked along a corridor, stopping in front of a big door. The two elves then turned to look at them.

"You will wait inside while we announce your arrival to the king," one of them said.

They opened the doors and gestured for the group to enter the room. Confused, and also not to cause unnecessary trouble, they did as they had been told.

Then one of the elves said, "You will meet the king when we say so."

Before any of them could react, the doors closed with a loud thud, locking them inside.

"What the...?" Dacey mumbled.

The three of them looked momentarily confused and freaked out, while Nadzia calmly looked around the room. All she could see were rock walls. The room looked like a small hall, but was completely void of furniture or ornaments. There was no window, and no other door either. The only way in and out was the one that was currently locked.

Xayvion turned to Faleece. "Would you be able to break down the door?"

'*I could try,*' she signed.

"Wait!" Nadzia stepped in. She ignored how hard their expressions turned when they looked at her. She *tried* to ignore the pang in her chest that those expressions caused. "We're here to ask for help, we can't cause trouble."

"They've just locked us in here," Xayvion explained in a condescending tone.

"Yes, I'm well aware of that," Nadzia replied drily. "But we need them and we can't mess this up, no matter what. Waiting for them to let us out and take us to the king will still give us a chance. If you try to get out of here by force, you can say goodbye to that chance."

They stood glaring at each other. Nadzia had been furious since the day before and it was finally showing. She preferred anger to hurt, so wasn't complaining. "We shouldn't do anything stupid."

"She's right," Dacey said, although she could see it cost him to agree with her.

Nadzia rolled her eyes and walked over to a corner, settling herself on the floor, legs crossed, her head leaning against the wall. She closed her eyes.

"Settle down, we'll have to wait."

Even without seeing the three of them, she knew they were all looking at her. Their eyes bore holes into her. Thankfully one of them seemed to come to their senses and moved, breaking the moment and convincing the others to find a place to sit and wait.

Nadzia felt like she could say she was almost used to being imprisoned, due to her recent experiences, but still wasn't good at understanding the passing of time. She was terrible at telling time when she had a glimpse of the sky, so there was no way she could do it in a dark room carved inside a rock.

She eventually fell asleep for a little while — out of exhaustion or boredom, she couldn't tell which — and when she opened her eyes again, Xayvion was walking back and forth on the other side of the room. He was losing his cool. She sighed and shook her head.

"Why do you look so anxious?" She asked him. "If something happens I'm the one who won't be able to get out of here alive. You are all fine."

"I'm *angry*," he corrected her, his brown eyes very different to the ones that had looked at her so tenderly just the day before. "We don't have much time left before a whole army of underworld creatures comes to kill everyone in the kingdom and the only allies we might be able to get are refusing to meet us." *We could go back and find everyone dead already.* She could hear the words he hadn't said.

She felt a pang of guilt and both her eyes and voice softened. "We'll get back in time."

He looked away.

They heard noises coming from outside and the doors finally opened. They jumped to their feet, ready either to fight or run. The elf soldier that had locked them in appeared at the door and *invited* them out.

They hesitated for a second then walked out. As soon as they stepped over the threshold they found themselves in a throne room instead of the corridor they'd previously walked along to get there. Confused, Nadzia looked back at the empty room behind them, then at the throne room again.

The doors closed behind them. Rows of guards stood by the walls on either side, and right in front of them, on the other side of the room, there was a big stone throne on an altar.

King Kagen was sitting on it, a crown of golden leaves shining on his head, contrasting with his dark purple hair.

"Come closer," he said. He didn't raise his voice, but they still heard him loud and clear despite the distance.

He studied them attentively as they approached him.

"You've come in the name of King Lucjan?"

Xayvion nodded. "Yes. My name is Xayvion. I'm his advisor."

Kagen didn't look that interested in hearing what he had to say.

"Two curious things happened today," the elf king started casually, a small grin making its way onto his face. "First, we have visitors come to us from Phexion of their own accord, secondly, they asked for *me*."

Nadzia realized they'd made a mistake. No one other than the elves was supposed to know that Eryx was no longer king. The others looked taken back. Xayvion was very clearly trying to come up with an excuse. In the end, he chose to change the subject and pretend he hadn't understood what Kagen was trying to say.

"We come with bad news, and a request," he said.

Kagen smiled, intrigued, leaning forward. "Go on."

"There have been numerous attacks on the villages near Lake Naraka and we have come to understand that it's something way bigger than we expected." Xayvion had prepared a speech, but now that he was finally talking to the elf king himself and trying to explain the situation, everything that came out of his mouth sounded chaotic rather than studied. "A certain Malkiya, a disgraced deity who corrupted himself with dark magic until he became a ghoul, has been pulling creatures out of the underworld and unleashing them onto the people of our kingdom."

"I don't see how that would concern me," Kagen replied, in a bored tone.

"He's preparing for war," Xayvion explained. "He wants the whole kingdom for himself."

"Ah, so you're here to ask for help." Kagen nodded to himself, satisfied to learn he had something they needed.

"We know we aren't powerful enough alone to fight whatever creatures and demons come for us. Which is why King Lucjan sent us here, to ask for your help."

Kagen's look was serious, but there was still a hint of amusement in his eyes.

"You want me to give you an army."

"An army, and magical creatures," Xayvion corrected him.

The elf king laughed out loud, amused. "Of course, I forgot how greedy you humans are."

"With all due respect," Dacey interjected, "he's a threat to everyone, not only us. He wants the whole kingdom and then some. He'll come to your doorstep as well."

"Then we'll fight him when he does," Kagen said, shrugging. "Why should we help *you*?"

"Wouldn't it be easier just to get rid of him all at once?" Xayvion said.

Kagen leaned back in his seat, making himself comfortable on the throne. "Having your kingdom fall wouldn't be that bad for us after all. If we survive this Malkiya you talk about, then we'd have it all for ourselves."

None of them had anything to say that would convince him it wouldn't work out that way. The elves were the only ones who had any chance of surviving Malkiya, and it made perfect sense for them just to wait it out until the entire kingdom they'd been wanting for years presented itself to them, needing help and guidance after a war.

"What would convince you to help us?" Xayvion asked, his voice strained.

Kagen's grin became even bigger, his reddish brown eyes glowing, making Nadzia's blood chill in fear.

"Well, it would be nice to know how you found out I'm king," he started in a playful voice.

Nadzia gulped loudly and prayed they wouldn't bring her into this.

"We heard rumours that your father had died," Xayvion said. It wasn't entirely the truth, but it wasn't a lie either.

The elf king raised an eyebrow. "That's funny. Because that information has never left my realm."

Xayvion tried a different approach. "You're awfully confident about your men's loyalty."

Kagen's face turned serious and his eyes showed a hint of anger. "Unlike you humans, we understand the concept of loyalty perfectly. I would be careful what I say if I were you."

Xayvion looked down. He hadn't been ready to confront Kagen. He didn't know how to get him to agree to help them. If he couldn't do it, then Nadzia would have to step in. She hurried to come up with a solution to get them out of there in one piece, possibly with an army.

Before Kagen could speak again, Xayvion found his voice.

"We'll give you her."

Nadzia's head went blank for a second.

Her? *Her who?*

The terrible feeling in her gut already told her what was going on, but her brain was still trying to catch up and process it. Slowly, she turned towards Xayvion who was cowardly keeping his eyes on Kagen, whilst pointing at her. Her eyes widened and panic began spreading in her chest.

"She's the one who told us you were king," he quickly explained. "She knows quite a lot of secrets about everyone in this kingdom, you included. All she told us was that your father had died and that you are now the ruler of this realm. If you accept to take her as payment for your help, you'd be able to make sure she doesn't give away any more of your confidential information. And you might learn about other people's secrets, as well."

Nadzia's mouth fell open, but despite all the curses she could feel on the tip of her tongue, the words wouldn't come out.

"That does indeed sound interesting," Kagen said. His eyes fell on her and he studied her from head to toe. From his expression Nadzia could tell that he didn't trust what they had said about her, but he could *feel* that she was different to her companions.

"I'll take her," he replied.

Her eyes widened even more and she looked around for something, anything. A weapon to defend herself, a person who could help her, something that could stop whatever was happening.

Everything was so confusing and she wanted to scream.

"Take her to the dungeon first," he ordered. Then, he smiled at Xayvion. "Let's talk about the details, shall we?"

"Wait," she said finally, panicking.

Two guards came forwards and grabbed her roughly by the arms. They started dragging her away, while she struggled to get out of their grip.

"Wait!" She looked at her companions. Dacey quickly glanced away and had the decency to look ashamed. Faleece was still looking directly at the elf king, unbothered. All that Nadzia could see of Xayvion was his back.

She didn't understand.

"Xayvion!" She screamed, as they dragged her away. "Xayvion!"

The door slammed in her face, separating them.

NAME: Hedyah
HEIGHT: 177 cm / 5'10"
AGE: 25
HAIR COLOR: red
EYE COLOR: blue
ENTITY: valkyrie

11.

The elves' prison was built in stone like the one in Phexion. The only difference was that three out of the four walls were made of stone instead of bars. The small closed in space felt surprisingly comforting, rather than claustrophobic.

Crouched on the floor in a corner of the cell, Nadzia hugged her legs and hid her face behind her hair, forehead pressed to her knees.

Once she'd been thrown inside the cell and found herself alone, it didn't take long for her to process what had just happened and even less to realize that it had all been planned.

'*You know what to do,*' Lucjan had said to Xayvion as they set off. Nadzia knew, now, what he had been advised, if not ordered, to do.

It had been foolish of her to think they were becoming friends, stupid of her to give in to her need for someone she could lean on.

She stifled a sob at the thought that it had probably been easy for them just to sell her out like that. Why did she even think a friendship could work out between them? They were from two different worlds. They'd never cared about her and they never would. They'd found out all the information they needed from her and then they'd got rid of her in the simplest way possible, dropping the responsibility on someone else so they wouldn't get their hands dirty.

Her nails dug into her flesh, but the slight pain she felt wasn't enough to drown out her feelings.

Hours passed and she didn't move an inch from her corner. Her body ached from the position she had been sitting in for so long, but she accepted it as punishment for letting herself get tricked and chose just to suffer. The tears dried on her face, then started pouring out again in an endless cycle. Her heart was beating loudly, her hands refused to stop shaking. Every time she thought she had calmed down and was giving in to exhaustion, the memories would make their way back into her mind, tipping her over the edge. The smallest detail was enough for the hurt to return and eat her alive.

There was nothing she could do, she realized. She was alone and in danger. She would end up dying in this world, far from home and the people she cared about. No one would know what had happened to her and the last thing she would remember would be heartbreak.

Lost in her own head she hadn't heard footsteps approaching. Only when the door opened and a guard came inside, clearing his throat, did she notice and look up.

"You're to come with me," he announced, "the king wants to see you."

It took a lot of effort for Nadzia to find the strength to get up and she stumbled a little when she tried to walk. The guard waited patiently for her. She followed him out of the dungeon, but registered nothing around her. She felt like a zombie, numbed out and walking on reflex. The guard opened a door and she walked through it without hesitation. He closed it behind her, leaving her alone with Kagen, in his bedroom.

He was standing next to a desk, looking through some documents. He glanced up with a smile on his face, but froze when he noticed the state she was in.

"Let's sit down, shall we?" he asked, walking towards the two sofas by the fireplace to one side of the room.

They each sat on a sofa, facing each other. She tried to sit as close as she could to the fire since the cold and damp of the dungeon had infiltrated her body and wouldn't leave her.

Kagen glanced at her cautiously.

"You weren't expecting them to use you like that, were you?" His voice conveyed a hint of softness, but Nadzia wasn't having it.

"I'd rather not talk about it," she replied, roughly.

Kagen nodded and leaned back, crossing his legs.

"Your former companions told me interesting stories about you, about how they met you and who you claim to be," he started, patiently studying her reactions. Unfortunately for him, she was too tired to react to whatever he was saying. "Would you like to tell me the story yourself?"

"I don't want to be rude, but I've already told this story multiple times and I'm sick of trying to explain myself when no one makes even the slightest effort to believe me."

"I'm more inclined to believe odd stories," Kagen replied. "And I'd like to hear yours from you."

She sighed and wrapped her arms around herself, in an attempt to give herself some comfort and the strength to deal with the subject once again.

"I wrote a story and one day I woke up inside it," she said simply. "That's all."

He didn't complain about her very brief explanation and decided to repeat what he had been told. "The world we live in is a place you invented, the people here are characters you created and none of this is actually real. Am I correct?"

She nodded.

"I don't know if you care about this particular detail, but you weren't included in the original plot so most of your world genuinely created itself," she added. "I had no hand in it."

"That's nice to know." Kagen glanced at the fire for a while, and when he looked back at her his reddish brown eyes reflected the flames. "What have you told them about us elves?"

"Just as they said before, I only said that your father had died and you're now the king. To be honest, that's all I know. This part of the story developed on its own, I didn't create it. I might know a little more about you, but not a great deal."

"And what do you know about me?"

She still wasn't sure that he was like she had planned him to be when she wrote the story, but this was a chance for her to find out.

"I know you're not how you pretend to be," she started. "After your father died you had to create a different version of yourself, to keep up his legacy. But you're not cruel or deceiving like he was. You just pretend to be, so you can rule the way everyone believes an elf should. You have a kind soul underneath all the layers you created, but you can't show it since it would undermine your leadership."

Kagen wasn't as good as he believed himself to be at hiding his emotions. His eyes betrayed him and Nadzia knew she was right.

"I'm just as you see me, no extra sweet, polite layers," he replied.

"You're wrong," she said. "You've already given yourself away more than once. Your eyes look kinder than they should. And just so you know, King Lucjan treated me worse than you have done, and I created him to be kind."

Kagen bit his bottom lip in the very first show of nervousness she'd seen in him. She could tell he was aware he was doing it, which meant that even if he didn't acknowledge what she'd said, by lowering his defences a little he was willingly *showing* her that she wasn't entirely wrong about him. It was a small victory and act of trust.

She opened her mouth then closed it again, not sure if she should ask or not. Not sure if she wanted to know, or not, but then gave in to temptation.

"Did their plan work? Did you really accept to help them in exchange for me?"

"I'll be honest with you," Kagen started, "I wanted to offer my help anyway. As much as I believe it would be beneficial for us to weaken their kingdom, I don't want to risk not being able to win against Malkiya later on. It's better to get rid of the threat before it actually turns dangerous."

"He's already dangerous."

"Not yet. Not to us, at least." Since the elves weren't Malkiya's main target, they didn't consider him a threat.

"When will we set off?" She asked, finally.

Kagen looked at her apologetically. "I'm setting off with part of my army tomorrow morning."

She felt a pang in her chest. "I'm not coming with you?"

"You'll stay here."

"What am I supposed to do? Wait in a cell until you come back?" She asked, looking upset. "What then? Am I to be tortured? Enslaved? Killed?"

"I'm not sure what to do with you yet, but that's a problem for later."

That's all she was. Not a person. A Problem. She wanted to cry again.

Kagen must have realized how she'd interpreted his words because he stopped and grimaced. His eyes were apologetic the next time they looked at her.

He stood up and said softly, pointing to a door on the other side of the room, "That's the bathroom. I guess you haven't had a bath in a few days. When you're done a guard will take you back to your cell."

"You're letting me take a bath in your personal bathroom?" She asked, surprised.

He shrugged and seemed embarrassed. "It's the kindest thing I can do for you at the moment."

He bowed his head slightly in an awkward goodbye and walked out.

Confused, Nadzia got up and went to the bathroom. Soaking herself in the bathtub was exactly what she needed to relax her aching muscles, and her heart. Her tears ended up mixing with the water and she nodded off a few times, too.

When she went back to her cell, a lonely meal was waiting for her on her hard bed.

NAME: Faleece
HEIGHT: 173 cm / 5'8"
AGE: 26
HAIR COLOR: black
EYE COLOR: grey
ENTITY: valkyrie

12.

Kagen was kind enough to give Nadzia regular meals, even during his absence. She was extremely grateful for that because one, she was hungry, and two, it helped her keep track of time.

When she opened her eyes again the next morning two trays had been placed on the floor next to her. One cold— her breakfast— and one still warm. She sat up and put the trays on her bed, making sure to eat as much as she could from both of them. She had no idea how long she would have the privilege of eating this well and didn't want to waste the food.

Nadzia tried not to think of anything, but her head still betrayed her. If it was lunchtime, it meant Xayvion, Dacey, Faleece and Kagen were already on their way to Phexion. It meant they were going to fight a horde of demons while she waited there, in a cold cell inside a mountain. Some of them might not even survive the war. Maybe Kagen himself wouldn't. What if he didn't come back? What would happen to the Elf Realm? He didn't have an heir, and there wasn't anyone else related to the royal family of the elves who could take his place.

What would happen to her? Would they just kill her to get rid of the inconvenience that she was? After all, she wouldn't be of any use to them. She wouldn't be useful to Kagen either. She had told him she didn't know anything else about him or the elves, so he wasn't keeping her to prevent her from snitching about them to anyone else. She wondered what exactly he wanted from her and why he had decided to keep her anyway.

She stopped and scoffed. *Keep her*. As if she were a pet.

After she finished eating she piled the trays and empty plates up next to the door. She walked to the far corner of the cell and sat down. For some reason she felt safe in that small, dark corner. She was far from the door and the outside world, and the darkness hid her from the prying eyes of guards or possible passerby.

Nadzia stared at the floor in front of her, absent-mindedly messing with the hangnails on her fingers until she drew blood. The burning sensation of the little injuries reminded her that what she was living was real. She was alone and she was trapped.

Her dinner arrived and she forced herself to eat that as well, even though her appetite was fading. Her thoughts were too loud to let her relax, so she continued sitting in her corner instead of trying to sleep.

Nadzia's weak heart had been getting fond of Xayvion. She had thought he would be able to help her, that he would gladly be by her side while she tried to understand how to adjust to this world. But he had abandoned her, and all for a stupid misunderstanding.

Even Kagen, who had briefly lowered his defences to show her she could trust him, had left her.

She shook her head to ward off the depressing thoughts, wondering what the others were doing. They should be traveling, maybe they were resting right now. She wondered if at least one of her former companions was thinking about her, or if she wasn't important enough for them to waste their thoughts on. Nadzia hoped they felt guilty. If she had to spend the rest of her life as a captive, she hoped they would at least suffer from remorse.

Approaching footsteps brought her back to reality, and she tensed up. She *knew* it wasn't time for her breakfast yet.

She glanced up and met the warm brown eyes she'd hoped she wouldn't see again. A fire started burning in her chest, another behind her eyes.

"Oh, you're here to sell me out again?" She asked, bitterly. She gave him a smile, but she was aware it probably looked more like a grimace.

"Sarcasm can't hide your true feelings from me," Xayvion replied.

Her smile disappeared. She got up and walked with heavy steps to the door, her hands gripping the bars so tightly her knuckles turned white.

"I'm not using sarcasm to hide my feelings, I'm using it to express them," she hissed. "I'm angry and I'm *terrified*. I wasn't supposed to be here, in this world, but it happened anyway. I've ended up in a world full of magic— which, by the way, I don't have even the smallest amount of— where everything and everyone could easily kill me. Where people treat me like I'm a freak show, like they own my life." Her voice started shaking but she didn't care. She didn't want to keep hiding how terrified she was of everything that was happening. "I'm far from my home and don't want to be scared every single day but *I am*, and there's no way for me to be anything else. I didn't expect you to trust me blindly but I thought I would at least find a safe haven with you. I thought we were working things out and that you'd started to care about me like I care about you. But you're just as bad as the villains."

Xayvion looked embarrassed, but his expression only made her angrier.

"One little thing and you abandoned me," she continued. "Is that how fickle you are?"

He chose not to answer, instead replying softly, "I'm not here to sell you out."

"To kill me then?" She could feel the bitterness and poison in her voice.

"Not that either."

She held back a laugh, biting the inside of her cheek and rolled her eyes in frustration. "Then why the hell are you here?"

"To let you out."

Her expression became serious. "What?"

A moment later Xayvion took a key out of the pocket of his pants and put it into the lock.

"I feel everything you feel and I can't stand it," he said, opening the door.

She scoffed, annoyed. Of course that was why... "So you're not letting me out because you did something wrong, but because my feelings are too loud for you? How noble."

Xayvion looked at her, his expression hurt. "That's not what I meant."

"What *did* you mean, then?"

She didn't care that he was hurt. He could feel bad and embarrassed all he wanted, but none of that would change the fact that he'd willingly offered her to someone else as an object of trade for a deal. It wouldn't make up for the fact he'd betrayed her and let someone put her in a cell. Again.

Xayvion looked at Nadzia, who was still standing inside the cell. "Aren't you going to come out?"

She shook her head. "I don't trust you. How do I know that you're allowed to open my cell? What if me leaving it gets me killed?" Her eyes filled with tears again. "My life might mean nothing to you, but I still value it."

"I know you don't trust me at the moment, and I completely understand why. We were supposed to go back yesterday morning, but I—" He stopped, looking away in shame. Taking a deep breath Xayvion continued. "I couldn't sleep because of what we'd done to you. I know how you felt when I gave you up to Kagen. I was never supposed to care about what happened to you but I couldn't shake the feelings off nor stop thinking about how wrong what I did was." If Xayvion expected Nadzia to praise him for that, he would be waiting in vain. "I tried to talk to Kagen. Dacey and Faleece went back to Phexion yesterday as planned, with a small part of Kagen's army." He reached out his hand, wanting to take hers in his, but she moved it just before he could grab it. He tried to hide the hurt it caused to see her back away from him. He didn't scare Nadzia, but she still didn't want him to touch her. If she let him touch her, she would give in to him, and she couldn't afford to do that. "We talked and I convinced him to let you go. You'll be free and he'll still help us in the war."

"I'm not truly free if I'm forced to return to Phexion with you to continue this suicide mission," she replied.

"If you have any other place in mind, you're free to go," he said.

She kept quiet. She didn't have a choice. Despite the betrayal and her uncertain future, she would still be safer with them than alone.

"Are you going to follow me out of here?" He asked.

Nadzia hesitated. "If what you said is true and Kagen accepted to set me free, then why didn't *he* come to open the door and let me out?"

"I asked him to let me do it," Xayvion confessed. "I wanted a chance to talk to you alone and apologize."

There was a moment of silence.

"You've been here for a while now, but I still haven't heard an apology."

Xayvion was taken back by that. Nadzia raised an eyebrow, waiting. Him saying how guilty he felt didn't mean anything to her. She wanted him to genuinely apologize because she wanted him to understand how stupid what had happened was, how it could have been avoided and how unnecessary it had all been. She was hurt and wanted him to notice it, to understand it.

"I'm sorry," he said eventually. "I'm sorry for how we treated you when you first arrived in Phexion. I'm sorry for getting close to you only to betray you. I'm sorry that I treated you as if you weren't a real person, that I didn't value your life, that I didn't value *you*. If you give me a chance, I want to do better. I want to be your friend."

Friend.

"I accept your apology," she replied, sincerely. "But I'm not sure I can give you the chance you ask for."

She wanted to give in to him, she really did, but equally didn't want to get hurt again.

Xayvion nodded to himself. He'd expected that reply, but was still visibly disappointed. "I understand."

He took a few steps back to move away from the door so she'd have free space to walk out. Nadzia hesitated again. She looked at him, then at the open door, still unsure as to whether she should trust him or not.

Her voice came out shakily when she said, "If I walk out of here and something happens—" She bit her trembling lip. "If you're lying—"

"I will go back and ask Kagen to come and get you," he replied simply, looking away in shame.

Without another word he walked away, leaving the door to her cell open. She ran a hand through her brown curls and cursed when a few tears broke free and fell down her cheeks. She walked back and forth inside her cell, her hands trembling. Nadzia was about to burst into tears when Kagen appeared in her cell, his eyes kind and sad.

"Come on, let's get you out of here," he said softly.

She nodded and followed him out of the dungeon and back into the stone palace. They walked out of the palace, into a big garden. An army of elves was standing in it, each with a magical creature by their side.

Nadzia recognized them right away. They were on the list of creatures she'd created but never included in her story. She remembered she had mixed two animals to make them. They were Caracals, but twice the size of a grown lion. Their abnormally large fangs stuck out of their mouths and their brown fur turned into black scales on their legs and paws. Their fangs and claws were both poisonous and they were beautifully lethal in more ways than one.

Seeing her creatures in real life replaced some of Nadzia's hurt with pride and excitement.

She forced herself to stop staring at the creatures and kept looking around. On the other side of the garden, standing in front of the elves was Xayvion, with his horse and hers.

"We're ready to go, if you are," Kagen said gently.

Nadzia took a deep breath to pull herself together. She couldn't just keep crying. She was heading into war and needed to think up a plan to survive it, or she'd never be able to go home.

"I'm ready," she replied, nodding.

Kagen smiled softly at her and signalled to his army to move off.

13.

Nadzia tried to hide her discomfort as she strode over to grab her horse from Xayvion. She mounted as swiftly as possible and rode away from him, while he just watched as she followed the elf army.

They traveled in rows of ten, the big cats moving in sync like machines. Nadzia tried to distance herself from the others, walking outside their organized lines. Xayvion was at the head, leading them all.

She couldn't stop worrying about what would happen once they returned to the city. Lucjan had ordered the others to give her to Kagen, but technically she was free now. Would he punish Xayvion for not doing as he had been told? No, that would never happen. Lucjan had never once punished him and surely wouldn't do it now, especially for something like this. Would he punish her for being there? That seemed like a possibility. Maybe he would lock her up again. Nadzia wondered if Kagen would support her if she asked him to help her survive.

She felt a movement next to her and turned to see Kagen approaching. He gave her a small smile and started walking next to her in silence. His cat looked at her curiously.

Kagen patted her head lovingly.

"Her name is Jaya," he said.

"She's pretty," Nadzia replied. It wasn't a lie. The way she looked and the graceful way she moved made her the most beautiful creature Nadzia had ever seen.

"I think she's intrigued by you," he continued, "she was the one that wanted to approach you."

"You understand her?"

"Most of us grew up with our cats. Creating a bond is way easier than it looks. I've had her since I was little." He looked at her fondly, scratching behind her ears. Jaya purred in reply.

"Why is she curious about me?"

Kagen finally looked at Nadzia. "She can feel something different in you. I've felt it too. Well, I still do actually. You feel different to anyone else I've met in this kingdom. It's like you're not from here. That's why the story you tell doesn't sound impossible to me."

She wasn't expecting a reply like that.

"So you believe me?"

"I'm not entirely convinced that you're the creator of this world, but I do believe you're from another one."

Nadzia tried to hide her disappointment, but at least it was more than anyone else believed, and a big step forward.

"Elves have a lot of magical knowledge right? Big libraries, old tales and all that..." She ventured cautiously.

He eyed her suspiciously. "We're not supposed to share that kind of information."

She understood that this was his way of saying yes without actually saying it. He didn't want to break the rules but still wanted to help.

"Do you have any information about traveling between different worlds?"

"I've never read anything about it, but admit I haven't studied all the magic I was supposed to. I'm not that much older than you and since elves are immortal, some of us tend to take time over our learning." He studied her expression. "You're trying to go back?"

"I've been here for almost two weeks and have no idea of what's going on in my world. I don't know if my being here means that I'm dead there. I don't even know if time is passing there or not." She explained. "I have no magic nor any fighting skills. This isn't the world for me. I don't belong here."

"I'll try asking around to find out if we know anything, but can't promise it will be useful," Kagen said. "If they realize I'm asking in order to help you, they might even choose not to share that information with me."

"You're their king, shouldn't they obey you?"

"It's more complicated than that. Rules and traditions are more important to elves than hierarchy. I would be betraying my kind by sharing such information with outsiders." He would be taking a big risk for her.

"You're still going to help me?"

Kagen nodded.

"Why?"

He eyed her, an eyebrow slightly raised. "Maybe you were right," he said. "Maybe I am softer than I seem."

She smiled suddenly. "You *are* softer than you look."

Kagen bit his lip to stop himself from smiling back. "It's our secret, alright?"

"Don't worry, my lips are sealed," she replied, pretending to zip her lips together.

Nadzia made the mistake of taking her eyes off Kagen to look ahead of her. Xayvion was still riding his horse, leading the army, but his head was turned and he was looking straight at her and Kagen. She quickly looked away, her mood ruined once again.

"Xayvion feels bad, you know?" Kagen tried to say.

"It doesn't matter. It won't change the fact that he still did it."

Kagen waited a while before he spoke again, debating if it was his place to or not.

"He rushed into my bedroom at dawn, my guards almost killed him in the process. He kept asking for me to choose an alternative, to think of something else he could give me to replace you," he said. "He kind of messed up our plans and we had to take time to adjust everything to the changes, but... that's not the point now." His voice lowered at the end as he realised he was going off topic.

Nadzia clenched her fists. "I'm not an object you can trade and move around at will."

"I don't think it was his intention to treat you like that," Kagen reasoned. "He was ordered to use you as an exchange tool."

The confirmation that it was an order from Lucjan didn't change anything, because she already knew.

"I understand that it was an order, and I know how loyal Xayvion is to Lucjan, so loyal that trying to get me out will likely cost him, both emotionally and morally. But that still doesn't make it okay." she explained. "He could have talked to me. If he'd told me what was going on and explained that it might have been the only way to convince you, I would have offered myself. I intended to do anything I could, anyway."

"You would have given yourself up for them?"

"It's not about them. The war involves everyone. Without your help we would all die, and I need to survive this if I want a chance of getting back home."

"Do you think you can forgive him?"

"I'm not sure it's a matter of forgiveness," she replied, confused at her own feelings. "Even if I choose to forgive him and try to rebuild whatever it was that we had before, I might keep feeling uncomfortable, and never be sure if what he says or does has ulterior motives or not. I'll doubt every little thing. My mind likes to play tricks on me sometimes so I might become paranoid."

Kagen opened his mouth to reply but she cut him off before he could speak.

"Please let's change the subject," she said quietly. "I don't want to discuss this any further."

"Alright."

He seemed to have nothing else he wanted to talk about and they just continued riding in silence.

She didn't feel uncomfortable around Kagen. Actually, she felt way more comfortable with him than she usually did with new acquaintances. The subject they'd just dropped, however, *did* make her uncomfortable, leaving a bitter taste in her mouth and an ache in her chest.

✳

Later, when they stopped to take a break, Jaya silently approached Nadzia, who jumped when she felt an unexpected wet nose on her arm. She found Jaya looking at her with intense but cautious eyes and stared back, unsure what to do. She couldn't explain her feeling as fear, because the animal didn't look threatening, but she was pretty big and it felt a little unsettling. Jaya nuzzled her head against Nadzia's shoulder.

"She wants you to pet her," Kagen explained, appearing next to her.

Nadzia carefully reached out and patted her head. Jaya seemed to like it and Nadzia relaxed, then started scratching her neck. The animal purred and stretched out her neck so Nadzia could reach the spot better and she chuckled at how cute such a massive, deadly animal could look.

"She likes you," Kagen whispered.

"I like her, too."

While Nadzia was petting Jaya, she took a closer look at the animal's fangs.

"Her fangs and claws are poisonous, right?"

Kagen joined her in petting Jaya and she looked ecstatic.

"Yes they are, but Jaya can choose when to release the poison," he explained. "She often bites when playing, for example and understands when she's faced with a real threat. If she feels she can't fight using her strength only, she'll release the poison. She's very clever."

"She sounds amazing," Nadzia confirmed.

She was starting to understand why Kagen looked at Jaya so fondly. The cat leaned forward and licked her affectionately. They both burst out laughing in surprise and Nadzia thought that Jaya might be the key to making the journey less overwhelming.

14.

Loud noises made their way into Nadzia's head.

A drill and a hammer.

The neighbors in the apartments above hers apparently weren't done with the renovations yet.

Cars honking.

Nadzia had always wondered why drivers always seemed most reckless and impatient in the mornings. It's like they did it on purpose to bother any poor soul who wanted to sleep in.

There was the sound of light music, too.

After the sounds registered in her head, one by one, Nadzia finally started waking up. Her eyes were heavy and wouldn't open at first. She rubbed them and gave them another few seconds to relax and open fully.

Nadzia sat up on her bed and stretched, yawning loudly whilst glancing at the clock on her nightstand, but it was turned off. She picked up her phone which was next to her on the bed, earphones plugged in and still working, but when she clicked on the button the screen didn't light up. She gave in after a few more attempts, making a mental note to have someone check her phone as it often just switched off, or worked in specific ways. It was frustrating that this time it had decided to block itself on the music app, but it wasn't surprising. Nadzia had been through the strangest things with her old cell phone.

She finally got up and walked into the kitchen to make herself some tea.

While she watched the water, waiting for it to boil, something started to bother her. Her brain felt numb, still clouded by sleep, and she couldn't remember what seemed to be bothering her. Her brain was sending her silent alarms but she couldn't understand what didn't feel right. Had she forgotten an important date? Had she taken a sleeping pill the night before and was still under the effect? She couldn't remember.

The sound of the kettle pulled her away from her thoughts.

The tea helped her wake up a little and her brain cleared, but the questions about the alarms remained unanswered.

Nadzia quickly washed and dressed. She picked up her bag and house keys and walked out of her apartment. She hadn't checked the time but she knew she was late for work, she felt it, so she hurried down the hallway.

She turned a corner too quickly without looking, and bumped into someone. A man put his arm around her waist to stop her falling backwards.

"I'm so sorry," she said as she pulled herself together.

She looked up to meet warm, brown eyes. She was about to apologize again, when the kind face of the young man changed. His smile stretched into a terrifying grin.

"You trust too easily," he said, voice as smooth as honey.

Before she could react, she felt a shooting pain in her stomach that took her breath away. When she looked down she saw his hand holding a knife, both of them were covered in blood.

"Poor naive Nadzia," the man mocked, smoothing the hair on her face with his other hand, "maybe you should have stayed in your own world. Everything would have been so much easier if you'd just minded your own damn business."

Xayvion's grin was the last thing she saw before he pushed her away and she fell like a dead weight onto the floor of the hallway, blood pouring out of the wound.

Nadzia's eyes snapped open, her body spasmed then froze in panic. Her eyes were staring straight at the stars above her and the sound of her heart beating was all she could hear. Her breathing was short and labored.

It took her a while to realize she'd just had a nightmare. She closed her eyes and tried to control her breathing.

It wasn't real. You're alive. You're still alive.

Little by little the feeling in her body returned and she could move again. She sat up on the grass that had been her bed for the night, clutching at her shirt, just above her heart. A tear made its way down her cheek and she forced her nails into her palm, hoping this would distract her brain from the emotional pain.

Finally her heart slowed down and she could breathe more easily. She focused on the people sleeping around her snoring softly, the cicadas singing and the light breeze blowing through the grass and trees.

When her body finally relaxed enough for her to stand up, she walked away from the group towards the trees. She needed some space for herself.

She heard a sound behind her and turned quickly. Flinching, she slammed her hand onto her mouth to stop a scream when she saw Xayvion a few feet from her. Her heart started beating quickly and loudly again.

"Are you alright?" He asked, looking concerned. His eyebrows furrowed, she knew he was confused by her reaction and the mess of emotions he was probably feeling from her.

Xayvion tried taking a step towards her but she took one back as a reflex, putting a hand up to silently tell him to stop. He obeyed.

"What's wrong?" He, too, was starting to panic. "You're scared. Why are you scared? Did something happen?"

She tried to open her mouth to speak, to say *anything*, but all that came out was a whimper.

His voice softened even more than usual. "I won't get closer if you don't want me to. I'm not going to hurt you, I promise." He put his hands up to show her he was disarmed. "I couldn't sleep and then your emotions started screaming all of a sudden. I'm only here to make sure you're okay."

Despite her attempts to hold herself together, Nadzia burst into tears. She covered her mouth with her hand to contain the sobs.

"You're worrying me," he said gently.

Between broken sobs and hiccups, she managed to say, "Nightmare".

His already sad eyes showed hurt and guilt.

"You were the nightmare," she explained.

His heart broke at those words. She could see it in his eyes.

"I'm sorry," he apologized quietly. "I'm so sorry, Nad."

She sat on the ground, letting herself break down completely. Xayvion watched from a distance, aching to touch her, to pull her to him.

"I'm not going to hurt you," he repeated, trying to make her understand, "I don't want to hurt you."

He saw her nod, but neither of them was sure if she'd done so as a reflex or because she really believed him.

"Can I come closer?"

Nadzia glanced up at Xayvion and, despite the tears clouding her vision, she could still see him clearly, in all his beauty under the light of the moon. Not even the black hair partially covering his face could hide his worried eyes from her. She nodded weakly. He walked towards her slowly and she watched every step, waiting for her fear to take over. Nadzia's heart tricked her instead, making her long for him the closer he got.

"Can I sit next to you?" Xayvion asked, once he was standing in front of her.

Again, she nodded. He sat down making sure to leave her enough space to breathe.

"Do you want to talk about it?"

She gave herself just enough time to calm down so her sobs wouldn't stop her from talking.

"I was back home," she said quietly, her voice broken and strained. Anyone who heard her say that could tell just how much she longed to go back. "You showed up, and told me that I should never have come here, that I should have minded my own business." A hiccup stopped her speech momentarily. She bit the inside of her cheek and wiped fresh tears from her face, making space for the new ones that would replace them a second later. He waited patiently for her to continue. "You had a knife and you stabbed me and then you left me there to die."

He flinched. She could tell he hadn't expected that last part. Xayvion looked devastated, which only made her cry harder.

Finally, he pulled her towards him and she melted against his chest. He put his arms around her shoulders and gently stroked her hair as she cried against him, fists clutching his shirt as if she were afraid he would disappear and leave her to suffer alone.

"I'm sorry," he whispered. "I'm so sorry."

Part of Nadzia felt cruelly satisfied that he was feeling guilty, but another part felt bad for blaming him.

"I won't hurt you," he promised. "I won't let you die, either."

"I'm scared," she whispered against his chest.

"I know," he replied tenderly. "But I'll always be by your side. You can count on me." He gently pulled her back and cupped her cheeks so she would look at him. "I'll make up for my mistakes and keep you safe, always."

"Can I trust you?" She asked, brokenly.

His eyes looked deeply into hers, so deeply she felt he could see her soul.

"Yes, yes you can."

She nodded and he pulled her to him again, into another comforting hug.

She hated how weak she was. It had always been hard for her to feel completely comfortable around other people, but she also had the bad habit of trying to give herself to anyone and everyone in the hope they would accept her as she was. She was a walking contradiction and hated how little control she had on her behavior around Xayvion.

"I miss home," she confessed.

"I know," he replied. "I'll help you find a way home. We're going to go back to Phexion, win the war and then take you home. I promise."

He kept whispering apologies and promises, holding her close. His strong arms made her feel safe, and despite everything, his words convinced her. Maybe she really was just emotionally weak. Or maybe she just really cared about him, way more than she should.

She must have dozed off between the tears, but was still half awake when she felt him pick her up in his arms and lay her back down on the grass. The last thing she felt were his fingers on her face, carefully wiping her tears away.

NAME: Kagen
HEIGHT: 182 cm / 6'0"
AGE: 27
HAIR COLOR: dark purple
EYE COLOR: reddish brown
ENTITY: elf

15.

Surprisingly, the wet tongue licking her face wasn't what woke Nadzia up but rather Kagen, quietly trying to get Jaya away from her.

"I told you to stop, she won't like that," he said in a hushed tone.

Nadzia opened her eyes to meet the cat's excited ones. Jaya finally stopped licking her, satisfied that she was awake.

"Good morning to you too, beautiful," Nadzia said, oddly in a good mood. She scratched Jaya's neck and the animal purred happily in response.

"I'm sorry, I tried to tell her not to but she just really wants to be around you today, I don't know why," Kagen apologized, glaring at his long time friend.

"It's alright."

Nadzia managed to stand up but she could barely move without the giant cat following her around, jumping in excitement when Nadzia looked at her and rubbing herself against her when she got distracted. Kagen had to physically restrain Jaya to prevent her from following Nadzia while she relieved herself in the wild.

Since it seemed the cat couldn't bear to stay away from Nadzia, Kagen proposed something.

"Do you want to ride her for the rest of the journey? I can ride your horse."

"Are you sure that's okay?" Nadzia asked, concerned. "Wouldn't your army see it as some kind of a betrayal?"

"It'll be fine, don't worry. Plus, I doubt Jaya will take no for an answer."

They put the bridle on and Kagen helped Nadzia mount Jaya since she didn't have a saddle or stirrups. When Jaya stood up, Nadzia almost fell off, but thankfully Kagen was there to catch her.

He walked around and faced Jaya, taking her big face in his hands.

"She has never ridden an animal like you, so don't make sudden movements," he instructed, slowly. "She's not me, okay? Keep that in mind."

Jaya was perfectly still as she listened to him. Only once he'd finished talking did she reach forward and brush her face against his. From Kagen's satisfied expression, Nadzia realised that that was Jaya's way of saying she'd understood him.

Kagen mounted Nadzia's horse and they waited for the rest of the group to get ready in order to set off again.

Riding Jaya felt different to riding a horse. For starters, her body was larger. The way she moved and the rhythm were different. There was no saddle so Nadzia felt her muscles move directly under her. It took her a while to get used to it, but she soon realised that somehow it felt more comfortable than riding a horse.

She heard Kagen chuckle next to her and glanced at him.

"What?"

He shook his head. "You look like a child who's just discovered magic," he replied.

"Well, I feel like one."

Nadzia stretched and straightened her back, then closed her eyes, taking in a deep breath. The sun warmed her face and the breeze brought with it the smell of grass. For once, she felt good, relaxed and at ease.

When Nadzia opened her eyes she examined the rows of soldiers and animals in front of her, moving forward in sync. Her eyes then landed on Xayvion. He wasn't riding at the front that day, but rather closer to them, somewhere in the middle of the army. Every so often, he would glance back to look at her, and this time their eyes met.

Jaya had distracted Nadzia before she'd had the chance to wake up fully, and she realised that because of that she still hadn't thought once about what had happened the night before.

Nadzia had let herself be vulnerable in front of Xayvion. In the middle of the night, after a nightmare when she needed comfort, it hadn't seemed like such a terrible idea. Now, she wasn't so sure.

She felt uncomfortable and awkward thinking about what would happen the next time they talked, and wasn't sure if she'd manage to be so open with him in the light of day. Would he expect more now that she'd let him near once, or would he understand her confusion?

She looked away, only to see Kagen looking at both of them. His expression was both curious and worried.

"Did something happen last night?" He asked. "I feel like something is different but can't tell what it is."

"Nothing happened," Nadzia quickly denied.

"Now there's no need to lie. If you don't want to tell me what it is, you can just say so."

"I'd rather not talk about it," she admitted eventually.

"Then I won't ask again," was his reply. Nadzia was thankful for that.

She leaned forward and petted Jaya's head and neck. The cat made an approving noise that was enough to make her smile, just a little. Nadzia leaned her head on Jaya's neck, playing with her fur.

She hadn't even realised she'd fallen asleep until she felt Kagen shake her awake.

"We're just outside Phexion," he said. "You should get onto your horse now and head over to where Xayvion is. The townspeople won't be happy to see an elf army walking through their streets and will need someone to show them everything's fine."

Nadzia forced her tiredness away and silently said goodbye to Jaya. When Xayvion noticed her riding towards him, he slowed to wait for her.

"The journey seemed shorter this way around," she said awkwardly to break the ice, and stop him from going straight to the point she wanted to avoid.

"The journey always seems shorter when you're going home," he replied.

She couldn't hide the pang the word *home* caused her. From his slight flinch, she understood Xayvion had felt it, too. He glanced at her apologetically.

She really wasn't in the mood to talk about her feelings, or about what had happened the night before, so she started moving again, leaving Xayvion behind. He soon caught up with her and they quickly headed to the front line.

"Part of the army already arrived with Dacey and Faleece, right?" She asked as they passed the people eyeing them curiously from their windows.

"A very small number," he replied. "They left earlier, while we delayed the real departure, as proof for Lucjan so he'd know the deal had gone well, and the rest would be arriving soon."

"Did they know why you stayed behind?" She asked, then specified, "Dacey and Faleece."

"I only told them I wanted to discuss some things with Kagen to make sure everything was alright," Xayvion explained, "but I think they both suspected it had something to do with you."

She nodded, lost in her thoughts.

"Why didn't you tell me?"

He frowned, not understanding what she meant.

"Why didn't you tell me what Lucjan had ordered?" She held her hand up to stop him interrupting her. "If he ordered you to offer me as a form of exchange, it must have been because he understood I would be useful as such— other than just because he wanted to get rid of me. I would have helped you with whatever plan you had, though, if only you'd discussed it with me."

"To be honest, I was going to ignore Lucjan's order," Xayvion confessed. Her eyes widened in surprise. Never in his life had he ignored an order from Lucjan. The fact that he'd even considered it was a huge thing. "It didn't feel right, and I didn't think we'd even need to. But then I started doubting you and when we were standing in front of Kagen I was taken by surprise and it felt like the only way out."

"It was partly my fault, too," she said, defeatedly.

Perhaps if she had told them about knowing sign language from the beginning they wouldn't have been so shocked, as that was what had triggered the whole situation. After all, Nadzia knew better than anyone that changing even just a tiny little detail could drastically alter a story.

"It was never your fault," Xayvion said eventually, his voice low. He looked at her and she saw the sincerity in his eyes. "You were only trying to protect yourself. There's nothing wrong with that."

She wanted to object but knew the argument would never end if she did. She wouldn't have had the chance to do so anyway, because they had finally come to the castle gates.

The guards recognized Xayvion and opened the gates, letting them in. Although the castle was big, it had already accommodated their soldiers and the elf army that had just arrived. The second part of the army wouldn't be able to fit as well, especially with the additional animals, so Kagen ordered them to wait outside until he had talked to Lucjan to arrange something.

As Kagen dismounted, the nearest guard tried to approach Jaya and tie her up somewhere, but backed off as soon as she looked in his direction. Kagen didn't hide his grin.

"Have fun with her," he told the guard, who looked like he wanted to stab Kagen with his sword.

The elf king followed Nadzia and Xayvion into the castle and the meeting room. The others were already there as they had gathered as soon as they'd had word their party had entered the city.

Lucjan did not look happy to see Nadzia and she realised that he hadn't expected Xayvion to disobey him. She also gleaned that neither Dacey nor Faleece had told him their theories about why Xayvion had stayed behind.

Lucjan's angry eyes rested on Xayvion and she felt a little bad for him. He tried to focus Lucjan's attention elsewhere, stepping aside so Kagen wasn't standing behind him anymore.

"This is King Kagen," he announced.

"You must be King Lucjan," Kagen said, his voice as sweet as honey, "it's a pleasure to meet you."

"Likewise," Lucjan replied.

Kagen's lips formed a tight line. He was disappointed. Maybe he'd expected a warmer welcome or hoped to banter playfully with another king to pass the time.

"That's it?" Kagen said. "I left my realm and traveled all the way here to give you my support and all I get is one word? What's wrong, are you too shocked by the fact that Nadzia's still alive and well and standing in front of you?"

Nadzia's eyes widened in pleasant surprise. She didn't expect him to jab Lucjan on her behalf, but made a mental note to thank him later since Lucjan's expression was gold. He'd never imagined anyone would mention the problem in front of her, probably because he didn't think she knew. Seeing her there, he must have imagined Xayvion hadn't even tried to follow his order, when he had actually followed it pretty well, only choosing to change the situation afterwards.

"He can be very hospitable, actually," Nadzia told Kagen, feeling a little wicked. "He let me stay in his beautiful prison when we first met. A real gentleman."

Xayvion silently warned her to stop it, with wide eyes and a small shake of his head, but she didn't care anymore. If things didn't go well with Lucjan, Kagen would back her up. He had made that clear with his comment just a moment before.

"We'll talk about that later," Lucjan said.

"Actually, I'd like to talk about it now," Nadzia replied. "I was, indeed, handed over to the elves, as per your order. Kagen, contrary to someone else, was kind enough to let me free." She didn't realise that she'd unconsciously phrased it so Xayvion and his actions weren't mentioned. Somehow, she was trying not to get him into trouble. Kagen didn't seem to mind her version of the facts. "So here I am, back to haunt you like a ghost so that perhaps you'll think back on your actions and wonder if *maybe* you could have done something differently."

"How dare you speak to him like that," Hedyah said, outraged.

Nadzia took a deep breath, trying to keep her cool. It wasn't really working.

"Hedyah," she started, her tone calm but strained, "I don't give a damn who you are and what you can do, or who *he* is and what *he* could do to me. You used me and then tried to discard me like trash and I'm not going to let that pass like it was nothing. If I have to be trapped in this world with you, I want to be respected at least."

"If you expect an apology from me, you won't get one." Lucjan's tone left no room for doubt. He was never going to apologize because he didn't think he had done anything wrong.

"If I can't have an apology, I want freedom." Nadzia wasn't going to beg for an insincere apology. It wouldn't change anything. "I want to be able to roam around the place without a guard, I want to train and learn how to fight, and I want to be included in your meetings. I'm still useful, I'll remind you."

"As I said, we'll talk about this later," Lucjan repeated.

"I'd like to hear this conversation, actually," Kagen said, a grin on his face. "I don't like the way she was treated either, so you know... I wouldn't fuck up an alliance that you desperately need if I were you."

"Are you threatening me?"

Kagen looked around, then back at Lucjan, his face and voice faking innocence. "Wasn't that clear enough? Should I rephrase it?"

Lucjan was clearly holding himself back from snapping at him. Hedyah, too. But as Kagen had said, they did need the alliance and couldn't afford to have Kagen change his mind about helping them. After all, he could simply choose to turn around and walk away, taking his whole army with him and no one would be able to stop him.

Lucjan brought the focus back to Nadzia, saying through gritted teeth, "You will have the freedom to walk around without guards." She raised an eyebrow, challenging him to continue. "And the chance to train."

"And, I will attend your meetings," she added.

"Don't push it," he said abruptly. "You can settle for two out of three."

Nadzia wasn't going to push her luck, not for the moment at least. Lucjan could keep his cool in front of other people, but he too had his limits. If she asked for too much all at once and pissed him off, he wouldn't care about the alliance anymore and just put an end to her there and then.

"Okay," she gave in. She could ask again once things had settled down a bit and he was calmer.

"Good," he replied.

Everyone else in the room seemed to collectively relax. Lucjan looked at Kagen again, no trace of friendliness on his face.

"Your army will stay here in the castle," he ordered, "if there's not enough room, the families of my soldiers will open their houses to you. We don't have enough space for all your creatures in the castle stables, but the townspeople have made theirs available to you."

Kagen's voice was sincere. "Thank you."

"You should settle in before we discuss business. I've instructed my soldiers to show you everything you need to see and know and we'll meet again at dinner."

"I agree, we should settle in first," Kagen replied. "Thank you for your kindness, I'll see you again this evening."

He glanced quickly at Nadzia and she realised he was asking if she wanted to go with him or stay there. She gave him a slight nod to tell him it was alright for him to go alone.

Once he'd left the room, Nadiza said, "If you don't need me anymore, I'll go to my room."

"You can go, but remember one thing," Lucjan said, voice low and steady, "you might have the elf king on your side now, but this is my kingdom and my castle. I'm the ruler here and if you talk to me like that again I won't hesitate to put you back in your place."

Nadzia replied by bowing dramatically to him, then turned and walked out.

16.

Not even the long, hot bath that Nadzia took managed to relax her. The more she thought about what had happened in the meeting room, the more she cringed. Maybe demanding so much hadn't been a good idea.

No, that's wrong. Nadzia had only demanded basic human rights. She had only asked for freedom, something she shouldn't have had to ask for.

She could, however, have broached the subject in another way. In a polite manner, for example. Nadzia had let her anger get the better of her. She'd never been able to control herself once she got upset. That wasn't new.

"But that's no excuse," she mumbled.

She should try and talk to Lucjan, to apologize. Maybe once the uncomfortably awkward feeling in her disappeared a little. It was better to try to create a bond with him instead of making him an enemy. They already had enough of those.

While she got dressed for dinner she couldn't stop thinking about the training. Nadzia knew she had asked for it but still didn't like the idea, although she *was* keen on learning how to fight and protect herself. But thinking she had to physically work to do it? No, she didn't like that at all.

A knock on the door dragged her away from her thoughts. When she opened it she found Dacey standing outside awkwardly.

She frowned. "I thought I could do without guards this time round? Has Lucjan already changed his mind?"

"No not at all, I'm not here to control your movements," he said embarrassedly. "I'm not here to take you to the dining hall. I mean, we could go together if you want but I wasn't ordered to control you—"

"Dacey," she cut off his nervous rambling. "Why are you here?"

He sighed. "I'm sorry. For letting Xayvion sell you out to the elf king and leaving you there."

"You don't need to apologize," she replied, sincerely.

The grimace on his face told her he wasn't happy with her reply. He looked like he felt really bad about what had happened.

"Did you know he had been ordered to do it?" She didn't really care because it wouldn't change anything after all, but she still felt like asking.

"I didn't know what the exact orders were, but imagined something similar would happen," Dacey replied, his cheeks reddening in shame. "I know Lucjan well enough to think he could do something like this, especially if it meant protecting the kingdom." When she didn't reply, he seemed to panic. "I really am sorry," he repeated.

"I know," she reassured him. "I accept your apology."

He relaxed a little, but still looked at her with caution in his green eyes.

"Let's just put this behind us, okay?" She said finally. "The more I talk about it, the more anxious I get. You've apologized, Xayvion did too. I believe that both of you are sincere and I really hope it won't happen again. Let's just look towards the future, alright?"

She realised while talking that she truly did mean it. Her anger about what had happened was slowly fading. She'd received two apologies and even though some of the people who were involved in the matter— and specifically, the instigator— hadn't shown any sign of being sorry, she still felt like she'd received more than she expected. After all, Xayvion had come back for her in the end. Holding a grudge would just be a waste of the time and energy she didn't have.

"I would like to formally be your friend if you think you can give me a chance," Dacey said slowly.

"I already consider you my friend," she replied. "I think I've considered you all my friends ever since I met you. I've known you way longer than you've known me, so I was already attached to you— to some more than others. Of course, some of you weren't entirely like I had imagined, but I felt close to you nonetheless."

"That makes sense..." he started, processing what she'd just said, "but none of us actually tried to be friendly to you without a motive. I'd like to try for real this time."

She smiled at him. "I'd really like that."

He smiled back and all the uncomfortable feelings seemed to leave him, his face and body relaxed completely.

"Let's go have dinner," she said.

Together they walked to the dining hall. From time to time Dacey looked at her and she could see the relief in his eyes. She was grateful he had apologized and wanted to be her friend for real, because she had started to become fond of him. Of course she had liked him as her character when she'd created him, but when she arrived in this world and realised how different he actually was, she couldn't help but become fond of him. They were supposed to be the same age, but she somehow felt as if he were her little brother. It was a nice feeling, considering she was an only child and had never had the chance to experience it.

Before entering the dining hall Dacey changed his features again. He was now shorter than her, his eyes were brown and his hair long and black. The birthmark was still there.

"Do you ever wear the same face more than once?" She asked, genuinely curious.

"There are some features I really like and find myself going back to sometimes, but I try to make up as many combinations as I can," he said. Then he grinned. "Confusing people is fun."

She chuckled. "I can imagine."

In the dining hall everyone else was just about to sit down. Kagen was already there, too, but he saw them from afar and waited for them before he sat down.

The atmosphere was tense and awkward, and Nadzia had no idea how to behave.

Thankfully Lucjan broke the ice by asking Kagen, "Is everything alright with your army?"

"Yes, thank you, they've settled in perfectly. The townspeople were really kind, considering we're intruding into their homes."

"They all realise that we're in difficult times. We can't afford to be picky."

Somehow that last part made Nadzia feel as if he was talking about himself and the current situation he had going on with her. She bit back a comment, reminding herself that she had decided to try and be civil with him from now on.

She tried to change the subject. "How did your journey go? Have you found the gold you needed?"

"Yes, we managed to find the gold. We hoped we would find more but it should still be enough for what we need to do, after all the weapons won't be in gold only," he replied. "The creating process is taking a bit longer than I expected. There are fewer blacksmiths than I thought in the kingdom, but they're all doing their best to work as fast as possible."

"We've commissioned swords, arrows and daggers, so they have a lot to do," Hedyah added.

"Mixing gold into your weapons was a smart idea," Kagen said. He looked intrigued by the subject.

"You elves have magic, but our soldiers are mostly human and they don't have any other way to fight," Lucjan explained.

Kagen tilted his head slightly in confusion. "I thought all your soldiers were human."

"Every division has a valkyrie as commander, and we're lucky enough to have a few other individuals with powers."

Kagen looked carefully at each of them. "No one here is entirely human, am I right? Well, apart from Nadzia."

"You can feel it?" Lucjan asked, interested.

Kagen nodded.

"Yes, no one here is completely human," the king confirmed.

Kagen waited a few seconds then raised an eyebrow. "You won't satisfy my curiosity by telling me what you guys are?"

"No offence, but I'd rather keep that information private. We might be allies right now, but we never know what could happen in the future." Lucjan looked at Nadzia. "Which means, you can't share that information either."

"Relax, I'm not going to say anything if you don't want me to," she said, rolling her eyes.

She noticed a flash of surprise in his eyes, but it lasted less than a second.

Kagen sulked next to her. Nadzia knew he didn't want to know it to use it against them. His curiosity was purely that of a child, intrigued by something new. He had probably already guessed Dacey was a shapeshifter but had no idea about the others. Maybe one day, after the war, Lucjan would trust him enough to finally tell him or let her explain their powers to him.

The rest of the dinner went smoothly. Kagen was perfectly able to keep the conversation going with harmless small talk. At some point Lucjan started looking less like he'd rather go to war than answer one of his questions. He even looked as if he was beginning to like him, but then again Kagen *did* have that effect on people.

When they finished eating and stood up to go their respective ways, Xayvion approached Nadzia.

"I'm in charge of your training," he started. "I'll come get you tomorrow morning if that's okay. We should get on with it as soon as possible since we probably don't have much time."

Nadzia grimaced at the idea. "Yeah, tomorrow morning is fine."

As soon as they stepped out of the dining hall, Kagen called out to Nadzia. The two of them stopped and turned around.

"I'd like to talk to you in private," he said glancing quickly at Xayvion, then back to Nadzia.

Xayvion didn't look that happy. He had probably hoped to walk her to her room and talk to her some more, but he couldn't say no to Kagen, so he just nodded.

He said to Nadzia, "I'll see you tomorrow then."

"See you tomorrow," she replied softly.

She watched him walk away, Kagen's eyes studying her.

"Walk me to my room while we talk?" She proposed.

"Sure."

"So.... what do you want to talk about?" She asked as they set off.

He looked nervous. "Well, I wanted to apologize."

Nadzia almost stopped in her tracks at that, her eyebrows furrowed in confusion. "I've received too many apologies in too short an amount of time. What are *you* sorry for?"

"When we were in the meeting room earlier today I got angry on your behalf, but after that I realised I don't really have the right to be angry. I accepted the deal when they first gave you to me, and I locked you up in a cell, too. I'm no different to them."

Nadzia was almost ashamed of herself as she realised he was right. She had honestly forgotten that Kagen had been a part of it as well, for some reason. Maybe it was because he had been slightly more polite than Lucjan, or because she felt strangely comfortable around him.

"I'm sorry for what I did when we first met, and I'm especially sorry for acting as if it had never happened." His voice was so soft and sincere that she almost felt like crying.

"I'm not mad at you at all," she replied.

"You should be," he continued. "If you're mad with them, you should be with me, too."

"I've received quite a few apologies now, and I'm satisfied," she explained. "I don't even think I deserved these apologies to be honest, and probably owe a few myself. I want to put this behind me, now. I don't want to be angry anymore."

He nodded in understanding.

"I just want you to know," he started, "that if you need help, I'm on your side."

She gave him a small smile. "Thank you, I appreciate it."

"I mean it for the future, too. If you don't feel comfortable living here after the war, you can come back with me. You'll always be welcome in the Elf Realm."

Kagen was becoming fond of her and Nadzia was glad. He felt like the first real friend she'd made since arriving in this world.

"Wouldn't your people be mad?" She asked, teasingly.

"You'd be a royal guest," he replied, shrugging. "They can complain all they want but wouldn't be able to do anything about it."

She chuckled and shook her head at him, sadly realizing they had reached her bedroom door.

"We're here," she announced.

She liked spending time with Kagen and felt at ease with him, but it was getting late, and she needed to get some sleep if she wanted to be able to function the following day during training, so they had to say goodnight.

"I'll see you tomorrow," she said.

"See you tomorrow."

He took her hand and kissed it, in a dramatic gesture. He was grinning like a child at the surprise in her eyes.

"Goodnight," he said, walking away.

17.

The training had been a bad idea.

Nadzia was aware she wasn't athletic but hadn't imagined for a minute she was in such bad shape.

Xayvion had come to wake her at dawn and she already felt traumatized due to getting up that early. He tried to build up her stamina with long runs, which almost gave her a heart attack. They did basic exercises like push-ups and sit-ups, then went over the self-defense training he had started explaining to her during their journey. Her whole body ached and she felt her muscles tensing up at every movement.

They continued until afternoon, then he helped her with archery training.

"If you're going to take part in the war, it'd be better to do so from a distance, hence the need for you to focus on archery," he explained. "Of course, I'll teach you how to use a sword, too, but you're unlikely to become good enough to hold your ground on the battlefield in the short time we have to train, so we need something safer for you, too."

He said it casually, but Nadzia felt like tearing up. It might have been her aching muscles, but she was fairly certain it was because she felt moved by his words. He wasn't telling her not to fight. He was teaching her a way she could fight alongside them without risking her life as much as they would be risking theirs.

"How would that even work?" She asked. "We don't know where the battle will be."

"You don't think it will happen the same way it did in your original plot?"

She bit back a smile at how casually he talked about her story, as if he actually believed it now.

"In the original plot the battle took place in one of the fields somewhere between Phexion and Lake Naraka, but so many things have changed already so we can't be sure that it will go the same way." She sighed. "I'm not even sure what will happen now. Malkiya has already summoned Cael and attacked the soldiers, which was supposed to happen a lot later on, and be an immediate trigger for the war. Instead, here we are still sleeping in our beds a week later, without any sign of where he is or what he's up to. Something's not right, and I'm not sure if it's gonna turn the odds in our favor or not."

"You don't need to worry," Xayvion reassured her. "We've already prepared much more than we were supposed to. We have the elves on our side and we're making new weapons. That's more than what was originally planned, isn't it?"

"Well, that's true..." she started, hesitantly, "but what if Malkiya has found a way to be stronger, just like we did?"

Xayvion's eyes were kind and fierce at the same time. "We're protecting our homes and the people we care about. We won't lose."

She wanted to believe him, she really did. But now that she wasn't directing events, nothing that happened was in her control anymore. She was inside the story and couldn't be sure they were going to win.

Heroes always win because writers make it that way, but Nadzia knew well enough that in reality it often worked the opposite way. Now *this* was her reality, and there was no writer outside it to make sure everyone lived to the end. She had to work for it herself and hope for the best outcome.

Xayvion and Nadzia kept up the same exhausting training schedule for the next couple of days. They met at dawn, ran and ran and ran again, did basic exercises, self-defense training, sword training, and then endless hours of archery. During the few breaks they had Nadzia was so tired that she could barely stand. Xayvion never commented on it, but he silently massaged her shoulders and back when he noticed she was hurting so much she could hardly move. Nadzia wondered if Xayvion had any other powers because his hands really did magic for her physical pain as he massaged her.

At the end of the day, Nadzia was always so exhausted that she simply wanted to go to bed, but Xayvion forced her to go to the dining hall with everyone else to make sure she ate well. Every night, when she went back to her room, she took a bath and then fell asleep as soon as her head touched the pillow.

And the following day, it was the same story all over again.

The routine kept her mind off things at least. She could only focus on the task in hand and, if she had time, on her aching body. She never found herself thinking about the upcoming war, or the fact that the days were passing and Malkiya was still quiet. Or even that she was supposed to be finding a way to return home. When she wasn't training, her brain was so clouded by fatigue that she couldn't think about any of that. She should have been worried that she wasn't thinking of all those things since they were vital, but was actually glad instead.

After a while she started getting used to the rhythm of the training. Not that she was suddenly athletic, but she didn't feel like dying every time she took a breath. Now, she had enough energy to chat during the breaks, and it felt good that there wasn't any trace of awkwardness between her and Xayvion anymore.

"How are you holding up?" Xayvion asked one day.

"It could be worse," she replied, shrugging.

"Is it hard for you to get used to life here? You said your world is really different."

"Well, I miss my computer and my poor curls are dying without the right hair products, but I can't complain." She sighed. "All things considered, it wasn't that hard to get used to things here."

Xayvion frowned and said, hesitantly, "Computer…?"

Nadzia halted for a few seconds trying to come up with something, then gave in. "I don't think my brain can handle an explanation right now."

Xayvion chuckled at her.

"I try to think of your world sometimes," he admitted, a far away look in his eyes. "I try to make up images of what it might look like according to what you've told us, but I'm pretty sure I'm missing a lot of pieces. It'd be nice to see what it's really like."

"It's such a completely different sight to what you're used to," Nadzia said, lost in her thoughts, "I can't even predict whether you'd like it or not."

"It's part of you," he started, quietly, "I'm sure I'd like it."
Nadzia felt a warmth in her chest. She didn't reply, but Xayvion wasn't expecting an answer anyway. She knew what he was doing, what the things he said from time to time meant, and she didn't know how to handle it. She wanted to lean into him, but it wouldn't be fair to either of them. So she just let him say sweet things to her and neither of them expected it to go any further.

✳

Nadzia was in the middle of a street, of that she was certain. It was night and the only light she had was coming from the half moon high in the sky. She looked around, confused, not understanding where she was or why she was there.

By the houses and the streets, she could tell she wasn't in Phexion, but in one of the small villages on the outskirts of the city. There wasn't a single light on in the houses, and when she walked around to inspect the area she soon realised that there wasn't a single person around either. The houses were abandoned, the front doors of some wide open, as if their residents had run away in a hurry.

The doors of the taverns and shops were also wide open, and Nadzia noticed the mess there was inside. Tables were upturned, the floor was full of broken glass and other objects.

The devastation around her and the silence brought her out in goosebumps.

What had happened there?

She turned a corner, and froze. At the end of the street, a huge black wolf was slowly coming out of one of the houses. But it wasn't just a wolf. Nadzia knew what it was. Or worse, who it was.

She also knew that it was already too late.

Cael turned his head towards her. He didn't give any sign of surprise at her presence. He slowly walked along the street, one paw in front of the other so gracefully that Nadzia had to remind herself that the creature in front of her was not a feline. He showed his fangs in what seemed a mocking smile.

Nadzia ran.

Her legs were shaking and her heart was pounding. She didn't know where she was going or if the hell hound was close or not. Maybe he was extremely silent, or maybe her heart was beating so loudly that it drowned out any other sound. She kept glancing back but all she could see was black.

She was so busy looking back that she didn't notice she was at a dead end until she bumped into the wall. Panicking, she tried to look for somewhere to go that would lead her out of there. Except it was already too late. The hell hound was at the end of the street leading to her. His pace slowed, as if he wanted to savor the fact that she was trapped and that he was so close to getting to her.

Nadzia's legs gave out and she fell to the ground. She needed to do something. Escape, grab something to use as a weapon, anything that could help her out in the situation.

Cael was standing in front of her. His unnaturally blue eyes stared into hers for a few seconds.

The next thing she felt were his fangs closing around her body.

Nadzia woke up with a start. Eyes open wide, it took her a few seconds to realise what had happened.

Another nightmare.

She curled up into a ball and lay on her side, closing her eyes and willing her heartbeat to slow. Nadzia tried to think of anything that would calm her. Xayvion's kind eyes were the first thing that came to mind. Kagen's sweet smile was the second. The feeling of Jaya's fur between her fingers and the way she jumped in excitement around her, the third.

Nadzia found herself smiling, her heart rate slowly returning to normal.

She finally opened her eyes again and looked at the ceiling. There was no way she could go back to sleep now. She would inevitably see Cael again if she did and end up having another nightmare.

She got up, slipped on a jacket and walked out of her room. Nadzia had intended to go outside and walk around the castle to get some fresh air, but she soon stopped when she noticed Xayvion sitting at a window, looking outside.

He turned, surprised to see her standing there in the middle of the night.

He smiled sadly. "Couldn't sleep?"

When she didn't reply he looked at her carefully, noticing how she was hugging herself. Seeing him there, alone and looking out of the window melancholically, she felt a pang in her chest.

He stood up and opened his arms. That was enough for her to start shaking again. She didn't think twice before running to him and he held her close as she started crying silently into his neck. There was something about Xayvion that was so comforting. His arms always made her feel safe, not afraid to let herself go and be vulnerable.

"Another nightmare?" He asked, soothingly, rubbing her back.

"Hmmm," she murmured. She wasn't sure if she could even speak without her voice cracking.

He held her while she cried and she just let him, needing the warmth. She felt guilty for wetting his shirt, but grateful that he was willingly trying to comfort her and calm her down. Never in her past relationships had someone seemed to care enough to want to hold her like this when she was crying. But she also had to admit that this was a peculiar situation, so maybe it didn't count.

When she seemed to have calmed down, he had her sit where he had been just a short while before and settled himself next to her, keeping one arm around her.

There was a hint of pain in his voice when he asked, "Was it me again?"

She shook her head.

"Cael," she whispered. "Malkiya's hell hound."

He nodded, trying to hide his relief.

"Everything's going to be alright," he said, "Nothing will happen to you, I'll make sure of that."

For some reason, his statement slightly upset her. "What does that even mean? You're a soldier and the king's right hand man. You'll have plenty to worry about once the war starts."

"I promised I'd always make sure you're safe, remember?"

She looked away, embarrassed. She couldn't ask him to do that, and she couldn't expect him to go along with it, but he looked so sure he could. She was more confused than ever.

"How are things going for everyone else?" She asked, trying to change the subject.

"Everything's almost ready and our soldiers seem to get along well with the elves. I think this could work out quite well."

Finally he let go of her, and she suddenly felt cold where his arm had been. She held back asking him to keep holding her.

"How's Kagen? Is he settling in well?" She blurted out nervously. "We see each other at dinner every night, but I haven't had the chance to talk to him properly over the last few days."

She knew, even before she finished the sentence, that it hadn't been the right thing to say. In fact, Xayvion tensed up next to her.

There was silence for a while, then he said, "You seem comfortable around him."

"I am," she confessed.

His eyes met hers, but she couldn't decipher the mess of emotions in them.

"What about me? Are you comfortable around me?"

The cautionary way he was asking made him sound vulnerable. She gave herself a few seconds to think of an answer.

"I was in the beginning, and I am again now," she started. "There were some days in between when I wasn't sure if I could allow myself to get close to you again or not. You were always one of my favorite characters when I was writing the story, you know? That's why I was so happy when I met you here. A few days after I arrived in this world I realised that all of you were different to how I had created you. The basics were there, but each of you were your own person." She smiled softly. "I like the real you even more."

Xayvion thought carefully about his next words. "The way you like me, and the way you like Kagen... are they different?"

"Yes, I think they are, but maybe not the way you would like". He looked at her expectantly. "Both of you make me feel comfortable, safe, and at ease. I believe I might be more fond of you than him at the moment, maybe because I've had the chance to spend more time with you, but I've strong feelings for him, too. I'm not sure what any of this means."

Xayvion looked glad to hear that he made her feel that way, but would have preferred a clear answer. He couldn't really complain, though, since he probably got more than he had expected. Nadzia didn't give the impression of being someone who liked to talk about these kinds of feelings so freely.

"If I had to choose, I'd probably choose you."

His head jerked up, surprised. Nadzia knew she was being careless. She knew she shouldn't give him hope. But she didn't want him to hurt because of her, and if that simple sentence could help him in any way...

"I think that if I were forced to choose, I'd choose you," she repeated. "But I'm not sure if that choice would feel true to myself. I'm not sure if that would be enough for me."

His eyes softened and he reached out to take her hand. She watched as their fingers intertwined.

"I'm sorry," she apologized softly, "I know it's not the answer you wanted." Maybe she shouldn't have said anything. Maybe this would only make things worse.

"You don't need to apologize," Xayvion replied. "I admit it hurts a bit to know I'm not the only one in your heart, but I can't say I'm disappointed with your answer."

He smiled softly at her and she felt herself tear up.

"You know I'll have to go back home one day, right?" She asked, her voice shaking slightly.

"I know," Xayvion confirmed. "If you don't want to go further and keep things like this, it's alright for me." He squeezed her hand. "This is enough for me."

She didn't know what to reply, but his expression told her he didn't expect an answer now. He was willing to wait and would be grateful for any little moment she was ready to give him.

She leaned her head on his shoulder and let herself enjoy his warmth.

18.

After the night she spent in Xayvion's company, Nadzia started feeling a little guilty.

She felt guilty for telling him about her feelings— however confusing, but real, they were— for fear of stringing him along without actually being able to give him what he hoped for in the end.

She also felt guilty towards Kagen. She had confessed, admittedly surprising herself as well, that she felt something for him too, something that was deeper than friendship and could develop into something stronger if given the time to do so. While she had confessed that to Xayvion, she was fully aware she wasn't being totally fair to the elf. In fact, she hadn't actually talked to Kagen in a while. While thinking about and overthinking her conversation with Xayvion, Nadzia realised she had been unconsciously avoiding spending time alone with Kagen. She talked to him normally when they were around others but as soon as there was the chance of being alone with him, she always had something else to do or was tired and wanted to go to sleep.

Despite realizing what she was doing, she couldn't stop herself over the next days, trying to be around Kagen only during mealtimes when the others were there, too. But Kagen wasn't stupid, and caught on quickly. He had tried to give her space at first because he didn't know what the problem was and didn't want to make her uncomfortable, but he didn't want to wait anymore.

That day Nadzia kept practicing even after Xayvion had told her to stop. They were supposed to go have dinner with the others but Nadzia felt strangely motivated to keep training alone— probably because she had just received her first weapons with gold in them— so she told him to go on without her. At first Xayvion insisted she eat with them, but he ended up giving in after making her promise that she would have something once she was done.

Nadzia practiced a little more with the bow, just because it was something she was already good at and liked the feeling of succeeding at something. Then, she reluctantly trained with the sword. It was pitch black outside when she decided to stop. Her muscles were aching but she felt satisfied, not something that she often felt about herself.

When she arrived at the dining hall, she found it empty. She wasn't surprised that no one was there, but it still felt weird to see such a huge place, which was usually full of life, so empty.

Nadzia walked to the kitchen door, her mouth turning into a smile when she noticed the cooks were still there. She asked if they had any leftovers or something else she could eat that wouldn't require them to use the pots and pans they'd just cleaned. The cooks prepared some food for her and she walked back into the dining hall with two plates, sitting where she usually sat with the others.

The silence was a little unsettling, so Nadzia tried to will her mind to think of anything that would distract her from the emptiness of the room. She was so focused that at first she didn't notice Kagen silently sliding into the the seat opposite her. She jumped when she saw him steal a piece of bread from her plate.

"Hi," she said, surprised.

"Hey you." His smile was supposed to be teasing, but came across as vulnerable instead.

Not knowing what to say next, she just kept eating.

"We haven't talked in a while…" he started, cautiously. "I mean, we have meals together every day, but haven't been alone like this."

She kept eating, putting more food in her mouth than she could chew, just so she didn't have to answer him. She nodded slowly instead, already fearing where this one-sided conversation was going.

"Have I done something to upset you?" He blurted out.

Nadzia stopped, surprised. The sad, confused look in Kagen's eyes made her stomach drop. Of course he'd think he'd done something wrong. Why hadn't she stopped to think about how *he* would feel?

"You haven't done anything wrong," she reassured him, quickly.

"What's up then? I feel like you're distancing yourself from me and I don't understand why." His voice lowered to a whisper. "Aren't we friends?"

Nadzia's mouth opened and closed in a feeble attempt to explain herself. She had to choose her words carefully, in order to not hurt him any further. She needed to be clear.

"I *have* been avoiding you actually," she confessed. She saw his face fall. "I was doing it unconsciously at first, and when I realised what I was doing and why I just couldn't bring myself to stop."

She saw the questions in Kagen's reddish brown eyes. He clearly wanted to ask why she'd been avoiding him, but was afraid of her answer.

"The truth is, I'm a coward," she said eventually. "I've been running away from my feelings."

Kagen found his voice again but it was a whisper, so much fainter than it usually sounded. "What do you mean?"

Nadzia sighed, running a hand through her hair as if willing herself to be honest. The air in the empty room suddenly felt icy, but her chest felt like it was burning.

"I like you. And I like Xayvion. I haven't known either of you for long but I know myself and that what I feel now is just the beginning. These feelings have so much potential and could become so much more if I give in to them, but I'm not sure I should." Nadzia looked into his eyes but couldn't read his expression. She was scared of what his reaction might be. "I don't know how much time we have and, even if we should get to spend enough time together to be able to figure all of this out, I will still need to go back home some day."

Kagen's hand reached out to gently take Nadzia's.

"I don't want to give either of you false hopes, nor do I want to force you into accepting a situation you don't feel comfortable with. I don't want to give one of you up in order to have the other either, and I don't want to be with both of you and then break both of your hearts. Nor do I want to be alone. I don't know what to do anymore."

Nadzia's voice finally broke and Kagen gently squeezed her hand.

"You can have my heart." His voice was sweet and tender and sincere. "You can have my heart and you can do whatever you want with it. You can cherish it and you can break it. It's yours."

"Kagen—"

"I mean it," he cut her off. "I don't care if our story ends in heartbreak. Even if that happens, everything else would still be worth it. Holding you in my arms, being able to spend time with you, being free to love you. It's worth it."

She was overwhelmed by his confession. Was he really giving himself to her? Nadzia found herself thinking that she didn't deserve it. She didn't deserve someone as good as Kagen.

"What about Xayvion?" She choked, unconsciously trying to give him reasons to back off and rethink everything he'd just said.

"The way I see it, you don't have to choose between us. In my mind, I always include him." He smiled shyly. "I like him too, you know? I think he hated me at first, but I've been trying to get closer to him and I think I might be making progress. Of course, I don't think he would be entirely happy about this, but I wouldn't rule out the fact that he could eventually be okay with all three of us being together."

Nadzia realised that Kagen had already been thinking about it. She understood at that moment that he had been fantasizing about a future where he could hold *both* of them, as if the fact that it could only be two and not three had never crossed his mind. Nadzia's respect for Kagen grew even more at that realization.

"I talked to him the other day," Nadzia confessed. "I told him that my heart was divided in two."

Kagen looked curious. "What did he say?"

"Like you said, he doesn't really like that he's not the only one, but he's still glad he has a place in my heart."

Nadzia stared silently at Kagen's hand still holding hers.

"In the Elf Realm we value our power and social status over relationships. I've never had a friend, someone whom I could trust, or even someone who cared about me. Not even my father cared. He raised me be to believe elves are incapable of kind feelings," he started. "I never thought I could be interested in anyone and I especially never thought I could find someone who was interested in me. You and Xayvion make me feel like I've finally found what I've always longed for."

"Do you... do you think we could be together? All three of us?" She asked nervously. "If not now, one day when things are better and we have the privilege of focussing on ourselves and our feelings?"

Kagen smiled softly. "I think that would be possible."

Nadzia's breath was ragged. She nodded at him but was mostly trying to reassure herself.

"Let's focus on the war for now, okay? We can't afford to be distracted by anything, so let's solve that problem first." Kagen proposed. "In the meantime let's just be ourselves and act however we want. Then we can sit down and have a serious conversation, try to explain it and put a label on it later, when things are better. How does that sound?"

"It sounds nice."

Kagen brought her hand to his lips and kissed it gently. He kept holding her hand even when she went back to eating, despite her protest that it made eating difficult. They kept that small connection as they spent the next few hours alone in the dining hall, mixing small talks with confessions, completely at ease with each other.

"You'd already thought about the three of us being together, hadn't you?" She asked him later that night.

He smiled. "I had."

"What did you think?"

He waited a while before answering. "There's a place in the mountains in the Elf Realm. It's a cave in the very heart of it. There's a flower there that blooms once a year." He glanced at her and smiled. "It glows in a way that makes the cave look like a starry night. I've only seen it once, with my mother, when I was very young. I told myself I would go back when I found happiness."

He wanted to go there with Nadzia and Xayvion because he genuinely thought he would find happiness with them. She squeezed his hand and smiled softly at him, holding back the tears that threatened to fall down her cheeks. The image he had offered her was so sweet it made her heart ache.

Nadzia so liked the way he talked about the three of them that she found herself wishing for his vision of their future, too.

NAME: Malkiya
HEIGHT: 186 cm / 6'1"
AGE: 400+
HAIR COLOR: red
EYE COLOR: gold
ENTITY: ghoul
        former deity

19.

That day Xayvion had other business to attend to, so he left Nadzia to train alone. She did try. At first.

Knowing Xayvion wouldn't be waiting outside her door to drag her to the training room enabled her to relax enough to leave her room later than usual. Without supervision or someone to force her to do the exercises, she slacked during her runs and archery training. She almost didn't try during sword training, feeling silly for pretending to have an imaginary opponent. She only lasted until lunchtime before she completely gave up and stopped training. Definitely not one of her proudest moments.

In order not to waste the day completely, Nadzia decided to take the opportunity to find Lucjan. She still owed him an apology after all.

She knew he had his own private training room. Given his abilities were different to those of humans, he needed his own space with special equipment. Nadzia knew exactly where to find him without having to ask.

She stared at the door for a full minute. Stepping forward, hand up ready to knock, she then took a step back. She looked around, nervously, but no one was there to see her acting so weirdly. Nadzia tried one more time but stopped herself again, running a hand through her hair and groaning at her indecision.

It was one of the few times she would find him alone… But was it a good idea to disturb him now?

She took a deep breath and opened the door with all the strength and courage she could muster. She had been so forceful that the door ended up hitting the wall, making her flinch. She quickly went in and closed it behind her, this time gently.

Lucjan was in the middle of the fighting ring, practicing his sword skills against an imaginary opponent. Nadzia didn't have time to absorb any other information about the room, or Lucjan in general, once she realised he was shirtless.

Toned muscles flexing at every movement, sweat making his dark brown skin glow.

He's not even real, stop staring at him, she told herself, her cheeks were burning up. *Those abs look pretty real though.* She pinched herself on the arm. *Focus.*

He brushed his damp brown hair back with his hand. Completely unbothered, Lucjan put his sword aside and picked up a towel.

"To what do I owe the pleasure?" He asked, sarcastically.

"I wanted to talk to you," she replied, looking away.

"Can't say I feel the same."

His words didn't really register with her as she was still very much distracted.

"Could you put a shirt on?"

Lucjan looked at her incredulously. "But I'm all sweaty."

"Just put a shirt on," she insisted. "You can take a bath later."

He sighed, grabbed his shirt and put it on. "Happy now?"

"Thanks," she mumbled, finally looking at him.

"Would you mind telling me why you're here? You wanted to train so badly, I thought you wouldn't waste precious time wandering around."

"I'm not wasting time," she said, although that was partially a lie. "I needed to see you. I've been wanting to talk to you for a few days actually, but never got the chance."

"Why did you want to see me?"

Now that it was time to apologize, Nadzia felt embarrassed. But then she thought of Xayvion, Dacey, Kagen... they'd all put their pride aside and acknowledged their mistakes. They'd all apologized despite being ashamed or embarrassed. She couldn't back down now.

"I'm here to apologize," she started quietly. "I have a few things I need to say sorry for actually."

Lucjan crossed his arms, tilting his head in interest, and waited for her to explain.

"I guess I should start with the most recent matter..." She forced herself to look him in the eye. "I'm sorry for how I behaved when we got back from the Elf Realm. I was upset, but I still shouldn't have behaved so disrespectfully towards you, especially in front of your people."

He looked away for a few seconds as if he were embarrassed at receiving an apology.

"I should also apologize for everything that I caused," she continued. "It's hard to explain and probably even harder to understand. When I started writing this story, that's all it was: a story. I know you're still angry at me for causing all of this, but everything I wrote was just for the sake of entertainment. I never meant to actually hurt anyone."

"But still you did just that," Lucjan replied, quietly.

"There was no way I could know it would happen," she explained. "All I can do now is apologize. I really am sorry."

Lucjan looked torn between accepting her apology and yelling at her with a list of reasons why he would never forgive her for what she'd done. From the troubled look in his eyes, Nadzia could see he understood the situation, and that yes, it was Nadzia's fault, but only to a certain extent. She could also see him fighting with that part of himself that needed someone to blame. Strangely, Nadzia found herself thinking that maybe, if he really needed someone to shoulder all the blame, she could be the one. It would only be fair.

Lucjan's expression hardened again as if he'd just remembered something. After a while, he said, "If I remember correctly, you said that in your original plot we didn't need the elves. Did we still win?"

"Yes, you did."

He looked confused and a little suspicious. "Why do we need them now? What's changed?"

This was what Nadzia had hoped she would never have to talk about. She was relieved when no one had asked about it in all the previous occasions they could have brought it up, but now she couldn't avoid it any longer.

"In the original plot, when Malkiya first attacked the villages, you were confident that you could stop the war

187

before it even started and just set off with your army," she started, carefully. "None of you knew who was behind it, or what kind of creatures Malkiya had by his side. You had no idea he worked with demons and naively thought you could win easily against him." Lucjan watched her attentively, his jaw clenched. "You did manage to defeat him in the end, but it wasn't really a win. More than half your army fell with the demons. The five of you survived because you're more powerful than average humans and because... well, you're the main characters and I couldn't just kill you off like that. It wouldn't have been good for the story."

"But you killed everyone else." He said what she didn't want to say clearly.

"Yeah, I did."

Lucjan looked angry and she couldn't blame him.

"You were just names, some of you were even just numbers on paper. You weren't real, so nothing that happened to you mattered in the end," she explained. "But now I'm here, and I know that this world is as real as mine. I can't just let all those people die, that's why I suggested you asked for the elves' help and thought of other ways to kill the demons." She made sure he was looking her straight in the eye when she said, "It cost you so much to rebuild all of this, the least I could do was help you protect it."

"Better late than never," Lucjan replied sighing.

Her last words seemed to have calmed him a little. He was still mad at her but was also starting to understand.

She took advantage of the moment to say, "do you know why I called this city Phexion?"

He shook his head.

"It's an anagram of phoenix," she answered, smiling softly. "Because when you had just fallen from grace and had nothing left, you came here, to this broken kingdom, and built it all back up, giving both yourself and this place a new purpose. You're the one who gave the people hope, who saved them and gave them a safe place to live in. Even if everything was already here before you arrived, it came to life thanks to you."

When she saw his eyes soften a little, she knew she'd finally said the right thing.

"Is that even real, or are you making it up?" He asked, voice rough.

"It's real."

He nodded. He lowered his head, looking at the floor, but it wasn't enough to hide the hint of a smile on his face. She unconsciously smiled back.

"I'd like to start all over again if you let me," she said. "I'd like to make up for my previous mistakes and have the chance to get to know you better. Maybe this time we can be friends."

Instead of replying to that, he suddenly blurted out, "I gave orders to check every book we have in the castle for any hint of travel between worlds."

Nadzia was taken back. "What?"

"I gave the order before you set off for the Elf Realm," he confessed. "I was told they couldn't find anything useful, but I'll have them bring the books to you in case you want to check them for yourself. Maybe you'll find something useful that we didn't know about."

"You—" She stopped a second, then tried again. "You tried to find what I asked for?"

"I'll be honest with you, it was mostly for my personal curiosity and to find out if what you kept saying was possible," he admitted, "but yes, I've been trying to find information ever since."

Nadzia warmed towards him.

"It doesn't matter what your reason was," she started, her voice showing just how vulnerable she felt at that moment. "Just the fact that you tried to find a way for me to go back home means a lot to me."

He nodded awkwardly at that, not knowing what to reply.

"It really means so much," Nadzia repeated, quietly.

"Even if we don't find anything useful?"

"Even if you don't find anything useful," she confirmed.

This time he didn't shy away. He looked at her and gave her a small smile. She had to hold back her tears.

"Maybe there's a small chance we could eventually become friends," he teased.

Nadzia chuckled.

"Just a small one," she agreed, smiling.

20.

The short heart-to-heart talk with Lucjan had taken a huge weight off Nadzia's shoulders.

She'd told him she knew how her actions had affected him and that she wanted to make up for it by helping them win the war with as few casualties as possible. Lucjan might not have forgiven her, but he *had* said he wanted to try again and she believed him.

Maybe, after all these weeks in this world, she could finally get along with her characters. She had loved them while creating them and writing the story, and wasn't proud of how she handled things since she'd appeared in this world. She felt the need to smooth things out with everyone and finally live the greatest wish of any author: being friends with their characters.

But not everyone liked her. Yet.

Nadzia noticed the redhead and called out her name before she even realised what she was doing. Hedyah turned around to glare at her.

"Can we talk?" Nadzia asked.

"Actually, I'd rather not."

She made to walk off, but Nadzia blocked her way.

"Look, we started off on the wrong foot and I'm well aware that you can't stand me," Nadzia continued. "I, myself, had moments when I didn't like you."

Hedyah rolled her eyes. "Shocker."

"The thing is, we're all officially on the same side and we're all fighting the same enemy, so why not put the past behind us and get to know each other?" Nadzia said, hopefully. Hedyah gave her an unamused look. "I'm not saying we have to be friends. I'm just saying that maybe if we get to know each other we might end up being on good terms."

"Me liking you is highly improbable," Hedyah deadpanned.

Nadzia smirked. "But not impossible."

Hedyah shut her mouth, realizing she'd just dug her own grave.

"You know what? I have an idea," Nadzia said suddenly. "Follow me."

She turned around and started walking, but soon stopped to look back at Hedyah who was still standing in the same place. Nadzia gave her a questioning look.

"Come on."

Hedyah was so confused by her sudden behavior that she ended up actually following Nadzia without commenting. Nadzia led her out of the castle, through the garden, to the stables. She opened the door of the first stall on the left and grinned at Hedyah before entering.

Jaya's eyes lit up when she saw Nadzia and she quickly stood up to welcome her. She started licking her face and Nadzia laughed, her heart filling with love for the furry creature.

"I missed you too beautiful," she said, scratching her neck.

Nadzia turned around to see Hedyah looking hesitantly at her from outside the stall. She didn't look scared of Jaya. She was more confused as to why they were there, or why the cat seemed to like Nadzia.

"Come in," Nadzia said. "Her name's Jaya and she's an excited overgrown baby."

Hedyah walked into the stall and approached Jaya. The cat looked at her curiously and let her close without complaint. Hedyah put her hand on Jaya's side and started petting her.

"I was right," Nadzia said with a smirk. "I knew you'd like her. You look like the type of person who would love cats, especially one this big and deadly."

"She's beautiful," Hedyah replied matter-of-factly.

"She is."

Jaya seemed to thrive on the attention, leaning in so they could reach the perfect scratch spots. Hedyah smiled unconsciously, and for the first time Nadzia noticed a softness in her blue eyes. Even if she hadn't managed to get close to Hedyah, she was still glad she could give her a moment like this, to relax and enjoy herself even if just for a second.

"I talked things through with Lucjan earlier," Nadzia said, trying to sound casual, "I apologized and we've decided to start over again." Hedyah looked at her, but Nadzia couldn't read her expression. "We've known each other for weeks now and all we've done is bite each other's heads off. I'd like to have a chance to become your friend. Even if I don't agree with most of your methods, I still think you're cool."

She was aware that most of Hedyah's problems with her concerned the way she talked to Lucjan. Hedyah looked up to him a lot and she had never liked how Nadzia talked to him, and rightly so. Nadzia hoped that letting her know she was working things out with Lucjan would eventually get Hedyah to soften up as well.

"Also, about what happened when we first met... I'm sorry," she added, embarrassedly. "I didn't bring Faleece up to offend you. I don't think I was really in my right mind during those first few days. I was still trying to get my head around the fact that all of this was real, and when I saw *you* for the first time I just wanted to tease you to see you react the way I'd planned you to in my head when I created your character. I'm not sure if that makes sense." Then she mumbled, embarrassed, "It seemed like a good idea at the time."

"It was definitely *not* a good idea," Hedyah replied.

Nadzia nodded. "Yeah I realised that too late. I should have expected you to feel it as more of a threat, to hear the name of the person you love coming out of a stranger's mouth."

Hedyah tensed. "I don't know what you think you know, but there's nothing between me and Faleece."

Nadzia looked at her, eyebrow raised in silent judgment. "Are we really doing this now?"

Hedyah tore her gaze away and focused back on Jaya. "I don't know what you're talking about."

"There's no need for you to deny it in front of me, I'm the one who put you two together, remember? I'm basically cupid."

"Cupid?"

194

Nadzia groaned then literally waved her hand as if to shoo away the 'cupid' matter.

"What I'm trying to say is this. I know you two are together and I support you. I *want* you to be together, okay?" She explained. "If you don't want to tell anyone, that's fine, but you don't need to lie to me."

"There's nothing between us."

"Okay, then explain why you're in the same division. There's only supposed to be one valkyrie in each division, as captain. Why is Faleece with you in yours, as vice-captain?"

"We're Lucjan's main division. We're the strongest and the ones he relies on for the most important missions. She's needed in order for everything to be balanced."

"Is that the official reason you used to convince Lucjan to let her stay there?" Nadzia asked, curiously. "You could just have told him you wanted to keep an eye on her to make sure she was safe. He would have agreed to it anyway, and it wouldn't necessarily have meant there was something deeper going on between you two. Friends can worry about each other, too, you know." Hedyah didn't reply, so Nadzia added, "I already know the answer, anyway. You're only making unnecessary excuses."

Hedyah stared at her in silence for a while, lost in her thoughts.

"Alright," she finally said. "You're right. Just don't go waving it around."

Nadzia felt offended. "I haven't told anyone these past weeks, why would I now?"

She shrugged and Nadzia finally realised how vulnerable Hedyah looked at that moment. She also realised the little victory she just achieved.

"Can I ask you something about this?" She questioned cautiously.

"I guess you can ask," Hedyah replied. "But I won't answer if I don't like your question."

"Fair enough," Nadzia admitted. She was pretty sure Hedyah wouldn't like her question, but she still wanted to try. "Why are you keeping your relationship a secret from the others? I'm sure you already know they would support you both."

In the original plot, Hedyah and Faleece came out and told their friends about their relationship way before the attacks to the villages happened. Of course the rest of the Inner Circle was happy for them and the two would then fight side by side during the war, focusing mostly on keeping each other safe. With all the events mixing up and creating a mess, Nadzia hadn't realised how the plot had changed in other ways too, preventing the confession from happening.

She was surprised when she realised Hedyah was actually going to answer.

"We know they wouldn't have anything negative to say," Hedyah confessed. "But we like the quiet we have now. We don't want any kind of attention on us, so we'd rather keep it like it is now for a while longer, until it lasts."

"I guess it makes sense."

She realised that they had probably found a way of making it work like this, feeling safe without any extra unwanted attention, without people watching them and judging them as a couple. If they felt safer holding each other in secret, that was to be respected.

"My girl certainly doesn't get bored."

They jumped at the voice, turning to see Kagen walk into the stall.

He pointed a finger at Jaya. "*You* are spoiled."

Jaya replied by licking his finger and his faked serious expression crumbled.

"That was your fault to begin with," Nadzia replied. "You spoiled her growing up. We're just giving her the love she deserves."

"And she's enjoying every second of it," he continued. "Look at that smug face."

He took Jaya's face in his hands and kissed her softly. Then, he looked at Hedyah and offered teasingly, "I knew Nadzia snuck in here to play with her, but I didn't expect *you* to do the same."

Hedyah shrugged. "Nadzia just wanted me to meet Jaya."

"Well, Jaya clearly likes you so I have nothing against it," he replied. "You're welcome to come by and spoil her, too, whenever you want."

Hedyah looked like she was about to reply, but was cut off by shouts coming from outside. The voices got louder and louder and were soon followed by other noises.

The three of them hurried out of the stable, just in time to see a group of shadows forcing their way into the castle yard.

21.

Soldiers were running out of the castle towards the gates that were being thrown open by the creatures. They seemed to be shapeless masses of thick shadow enveloped in banks of mist, but looking closely Nadzia could see something resembling a face in the darkness. Hysterical, high pitched laughter resounded through the yard.

Hedyah didn't waste a second and threw herself between the shadows and the soldiers.

Nadzia was in shock and felt completely lost. She took a step forward, not knowing what to do exactly. She felt a hand grip her wrist, forcing her attention elsewhere. Kagen's face was worried.

"Go back inside," he said quickly. "You've been practicing with the bow, right? Go inside and join the archers." She opened her mouth to reply, but he cut her off. "Go!"

Nadzia started running and he watched her anxiously as she entered the castle. He wanted to make sure she was inside before he dove into battle as well.

She felt like a fish trying to swim upstream, running along the corridors and making her way through all the soldiers running in the opposite direction. Her heart was beating so loud she could feel it in her ears. The frenzy around her didn't help her nerves. Everyone there already had experience in battles and probably wars, too. So why did *they* all look so *worried*?

Reaching the roof, Nadzia grabbed a bow and a quiver of newly made arrows. She looked around for somewhere to stand, finding a place right in front of the entrance to the castle garden.

Taking an arrow, she placed it against her bow and looked around, finally noticing how dark everything seemed. The sky was cloudy, making it harder to see, but the shadows looked as if they had all melted together because of the dark mist around them, enveloping the fighting soldiers. Despite looking as if they had no bodies, they clawed their way through the soldiers with shadow talons, leaving them screaming as if burned.

Nadzia started panicking, her hands shaking. How was she supposed to kill the shadows like this? She couldn't see clearly. What if she accidentally shot one of their soldiers? She hadn't trained enough, she couldn't possibly manage in a situation like this. She wasn't ready. She wasn't like them, she couldn't fight the way they expected her to.

"Get a grip!" Shouted the archer to her right, while firing his arrow.

He glared at her wide-eyed, panicky expression and grabbed the arrow from her hands, placing it on his bow. That seemed to wake her up from her trance.

She shouldn't be freaking out. She had trained, and Faleece had told her she was a natural. She could do it. She simply had to keep calm, although that would probably be the hardest part.

Grabbing another arrow from the quiver, Nadzia took up her position again. She breathed deeply in and out and her head started to feel clearer.

In the tangle of darkness and human bodies she saw Hedyah, who had somehow found a sword and was fighting against a number of shadows at once, so many Nadzia couldn't count them all. They looked like one and many more at the same time.

She pointed, fired and hoped.

There was a screech and then one of the shadows in front of Hedyah disappeared. Nadzia forced herself not to think of the fact that she had succeeded and just kept firing. She'd have time to celebrate later.

Someone had let the elves' cats out of the stables and they were attacking the shadows, sinking their fangs into the mist and squashing them with their paws.

Nadzia noticed how the soldiers were trying to make their way to the gate to run into the city and protect the citizens. She couldn't hear any screams from the city, but that didn't mean people weren't in danger. So Nadzia focused on shooting the shadows blocking their way, to make sure the soldiers could check that people outside the castle walls were safe. The creatures were fast and mostly incorporeal, and sometimes Nadzia's arrows only brushed against the mist around them. Most of the time, however, her arrows hit their targets.

When the gates were clear enough, the soldiers flooded out onto the streets. Both Hedyah and Kagen stayed in the yard, together with the cats and the many soldiers who were appearing from other parts of the castle.

From then on, Nadzia made it her mission to check on Hedyah and Kagen and kill as many shadows around them as she could. She could swear she saw Kagen look up at the castle with a smirk on his face for a few seconds before he went back to fighting.

A shadow clawed Jaya and she stepped back with a pained whine. Nadzia took the chance to fire at the shadow that was about to jump on the animal, killing it before it reached her. Jaya recovered a few seconds later and jumped onto another shadow that was attacking a soldier.

Nadzia could smell blood from where she was, but wasn't sure if it was the real smell or if her brain was tricking her. There was another smell in the air too, a sharp acid smell, which she imagined was emanating from the dying shadows.

Her breath was ragged and her mind couldn't keep up with her body anymore. It moved and fired on its own, on instinct, hoping it would hit the right target.

Out of the corner of her eye she saw Jaya jump to bite two shadows that were trying to attack Kagen from behind. He was startled by Jaya, thinking she was injured and quickly turned to assist her. That moment of distraction was enough for the shadows to attack and sink their talons into Kagen's side.

Nadzia gasped, her heart skipping a beat. Her body moved quickly and shot an arrow, killing the creature. Thankfully Jaya was quick to act and shielded Kagen with her body, giving him something to lean on while she dealt with the enemies around them.

Switching quiver after quiver and shooting arrow after arrow, the number of shadows finally seemed to drop until there were so few that the cats could take them all out in one blow.

Nadzia didn't wait for instructions from the other archers, nor to see if any more shadows would be coming or not. She threw her bow aside and ran down the stairs. The hallways of the castle had never seemed longer than at that moment. She felt as if she were in a maze, unable to find the exit.

Kagen *had to* be alright. She couldn't lose him. Not like that.

She came to the door at long last and sprinted outside, where the soldiers were helping each other stand. But Nadzia couldn't care less about them. She ran straight to Kagen, who was still leaning against Jaya, holding his side. His shirt was red with blood.

In a second her hands were on him, checking for other injuries and how serious they were. Kagen's hands grabbed her wrists, stopping her.

"Nadzia!"

She paused and realised he had been calling her name for a while.

"Are you alright?" He asked. "Are you hurt?"

She couldn't believe it. He had blood all over his shirt and was asking about her.

"*You* are the one who's hurt!" She almost yelled.

"I'm fine," he replied, trying to calm her down.

"No, you're hurt."

She was going crazy. If he didn't let go of her hands soon and let her see for herself, she would lose it completely.

As if he'd heard her thoughts, he lifted his bloodied shirt for her to see.

"I'm fine," he repeated, this time softly.

She looked down and choked on a sob. Where a big gash was supposed to be, only a thin scar remained, with a bit of blood staining his pale skin. Had she imagined him being attacked? No, the blood on his shirt and the scar were proof that he had been injured.

It took her a while to realise why he wasn't hurt, and she was ashamed that she'd forgotten such an important piece of information. Maybe the shock of what had just happened was getting to her.

"If the injury is not fatal we can heal ourselves," he explained, letting go of her hands. "We just need a few moments to get back on track. I admit that injury burnt a little more than it was supposed to, though."

"You— you're okay?" She asked, voice shaking. She needed him to tell her, just to make sure.

He nodded. "I'm okay."

She let out a relieved breath and felt her legs give way, all the adrenaline finally leaving her. Kagen caught her just in time and helped her sit down on the ground.

He was okay. Kagen was okay. Not injured. Safe.

He gently moved a strand of hair off her face. "What about you? Are you alright?"

She nodded, not trusting herself to speak.

She saw him look around, to assess the damage. Some soldiers were down but looked as if they were still breathing.

Hedyah was alright and was helping some of the soldiers back inside the castle.

Now that the worst was over, the reality of what had happened hit her and she was overcome by the fear she had forced away during the battle.

"You were amazing," Kagen said, squeezing her hand. "You saved us today."

It wasn't entirely true. She hadn't saved them, but she had helped. She didn't have the energy to argue, though, so she stayed quiet.

Nadzia felt Jaya nudge her and she looked up. There were two cuts right above her eyes. A few centimeters lower and the shadow could have gouged her eye out. Jaya whined a little when Nadzia tried to pet her.

"We'll get her treated, don't worry," Kagen reassured her. "She's been through worse. She's a warrior, remember?"

Nadzia must have nodded because Kagen looked relieved. He caught Nadzia's attention again when he leaned forward and took her arm, putting it around his shoulders.

"Let's get you inside, okay?"

He helped her get back up, her legs still visibly shaking. Thankfully he was strong and carried her into the castle, setting her down somewhere, although her surroundings didn't really register in her head. She barely even noticed Lucjan when he strode past her towards the hall where the injured were being taken, and completely missed Dacey as he ran down the hallway and turned into a bird mid-run to fly out of the castle.

22.

Nadzia saw people walking past her as if they were moving in fast motion. It reminded her of the scenes she'd seen in movies when a character stands still, while the rest of the world keeps living, unbothered. She felt a laugh build up inside her at the ridiculousness of it all.

She was aware of Kagen's presence. He stayed by her side most of the time, getting up every so often to talk to someone. Nadzia couldn't see who. Or maybe she just couldn't move her head to look at them properly.

She understood that Kagen talked to her, too, but his words were muffled as if she were underwater. The only thing she was aware of was his hand on hers. The warmth of his touch was probably the only thing keeping her anchored to reality.

She didn't know how much time she'd spent sitting there frozen, but at some stage she started feeling the pain in her back muscles, which slowly made the haze in her brain disappear. Kagen felt the change and turned completely towards her, watching her attentively.

"Nadzia?"

When her eyes met his, he let out a huge relieved sigh and smiled nervously.

"Hey," he said softly, rubbing his thumb on her hand soothingly. "Are you feeling a little better?"

"I'm not sure," she replied, voice strained.

He nodded in understanding.

"How is everyone else? Are they hurt?" She asked, finally looking around. She was sitting by a window right outside the dining hall. The doors of the hall were open and she could see the soldiers either sitting or laying on the tables, resting while healers walked around amongst them and checked their injuries.

"No one died," he started. "Many of the soldiers were injured but none of them too seriously, they'll recover soon. The shadows have attacked some parts of the city, but they seem to have focused mainly on the castle. Lucjan thinks they were only sent to scare us, or to try to weaken us, considering their relatively low numbers."

Low numbers... If that many creatures weren't considered a lot, she didn't want to find out what a high number looked like.

"Lucjan has sent Dacey to scout the enemy. We need to know where they are, if they're coming for us and what their numbers are," he continued. "Hedyah and Faleece are both okay. They're helping the injured right now."

The fact that one name was missing from Kagen's report set an alarm off in Nadzia's brain.

"What about Xayvion?" She asked, worried. "What about him? Where is he?"

Kagen hesitated a second. "He should have been out of the city when the attack happened. He's not back yet."

Her eyes were burning with unshed tears. "What if something's happened to him?"

"He's alright," Kagen promised her. "Lucjan said that if something serious had happened to Xayvion he would know. He said he would feel it."

That was enough to assure her that he wasn't dead, but not enough to calm her down.

"But what if he's badly injured? We should go look for him." She made to get up but Kagen kept her still.

"Lucjan's already sent someone."

"I should go as well."

Again, she tried to get up but Kagen gently made her sit down again.

"I know you're worried about him, but you're still in shock. You really shouldn't go anywhere." His voice was harsh and soft in equal measure. "You should rest and recover your strength."

"I'm fine," she lied, her weak voice betraying her.

"Nadzia, please," he begged her, "please rest."

She finally looked at him properly and noticed that his normally perfectly styled dark purple hair was messy as if he'd run his hands through it repeatedly and couldn't bother fixing it. His eyes were full of worry and they were staring directly into hers.

"Please rest," he repeated in a whisper.

"I want to wait for Xayvion," she said softly. "I want to wait for Xayvion at the door."

Knowing that nothing he could say would make her change her mind, he sighed and nodded. He took a blanket and wrapped it around her, then helped her up and together they walked to the entrance of the castle. They sat side by side on the steps, facing the open gates.

Kagen wrapped an arm around her, for warmth and comfort.

"He'll be okay," he murmured. "He's a strong warrior, and he most likely wasn't even around when this mess happened."

Nadzia just nodded. She was grateful to Kagen who was trying to reassure her, but it wasn't really working. She tried to focus on something else.

"Thank you for taking care of me," she whispered.

He smiled gently. "You saved both me and Jaya more than once from up there today, it's the least I can do." His smile grew bigger when he noticed her flustered reaction. "I know you've been training but I never imagined you'd be that good already."

"Faleece said I have natural talent," she replied. "Only regarding archery, though. I'm a mess at everything else."

"At least it's a talent that will be useful in this world."

She gave a small shrug. It might be a talent, and it might help her survive, but she wasn't happy with the idea she would be using it to kill. She wasn't really sure how she felt about that. She didn't feel guilty, but had a weight on her chest either way. The shadows and demons weren't human beings. She could say they weren't living creatures, either. But destroying them still counted as killing, didn't it?

Sitting on the stairs in silence, they watched people walking in and out of the castle, who in return gave them strange, confused looks. They watched the sunset and the sky turn dark. The more time passed, the more the weight on Nadzia's chest became painful.

'I'm sorry,' she wanted to tell him. She had no idea what was going on with her, why she was falling apart so easily. Kagen had been so sweet to her ever since they'd met, and even more so since they'd talked about their situation. He seemed to genuinely care for her and she was simply being a burden. She wanted to apologize to him, but for some reason the apology didn't feel right. Most importantly she wanted to stop being fragile, but she had no idea how. Giving in to her sad feelings was so much easier and something she was used to doing.

The sudden sound of hooves was enough to make Nadzia flinch. She stood up quickly, waiting for the horse to reach the entrance. Finally, it appeared, and Nadzia let out a sigh of relief when she saw who was riding it.

Her relief turned to worry, however, when Xayvion dismounted the horse with a groan and limped forwards. He finally noticed Nadzia when she started running towards him, throwing her blanket on the ground.

"What happened to you?" Her voice was shaking with worry.

He gave her a small smile and put a hand on her arm, trying to calm her down. "It's just a few scratches, I'm alright."

"No, no, you're not," she said, shaking her head. "You need to get them checked."

Before Xayvion could reply, Kagen stepped forward and took his horse's reins. He gave Xayvion a look Nadzia didn't understand and said, "I'll take the horse to the stables. Get your injuries treated."

Kagen walked away with the horse and Nadzia quickly stepped forward and put Xayvion's arm around her shoulders.

"I can walk," he said quietly.

"Just to be sure," she replied. She felt his eyes on her but couldn't find the courage to look up at his face.

They went into the castle and Nadzia quickly stopped to steal one of the healing kits from the dining— now hospital— hall. She wanted some calm and privacy so instead of leading him in there, she walked him to her bedroom.

Nadzia took a chair into the bathroom and had Xayvion sit on it. She looked away, then back at him, awkwardly picking at her hands. Now that she was there she didn't know where to start to help him. She needed to get a grip. The worst part was over, so why was she still so anxious?

"I need to know where you're hurt," she mumbled.

He leaned down and rolled up his pants to expose a cut on his leg. Nadzia knelt in front of him and started inspecting and treating the cut. Xayvion watched her silently, a worried expression on his face.

"What happened here?" He asked, cautiously.

"Shadow creatures attacked the castle," she replied weakly. "I'm not sure how much damage they did to the rest of the city, I've been a little out of it for the last few hours."

"Where were you during the attack?"

"With the archers."

Xayvion was surprised. He'd expected to hear that she had hidden somewhere. Not because he believed she was a coward, but rather because he hadn't thought she was emotionally ready to fight and that the sudden attack might have surprised her too much to be able to act. It had, in fact, been like that in a way. She had panicked at first but somehow still managed to act. And she hadn't been mentally ready to fight, which was why she was acting strangely now. Her brain didn't seem to want to fully process all that had happened in the last hours.

She stopped working on his injury when his hand gently cupped her cheek and made her look up at him.

"I'm proud of you."

Xayvion leaned forward to leave a gentle kiss on her forehead. A tear finally broke free from her eye and he wiped it away. She loved it when he was casually affectionate, it made her feel more important and cared for than any word could ever do.

"I was terrified," she admitted, comfortable with being vulnerable in front of him. "I still am, actually. I feel very confused."

"It's normal to feel that way. You weren't ready for it," Xayvion replied, his eyes turning sad. "You can never be ready for a real fight."

She leaned into the warmth of his hand and closed her eyes, letting herself relax for a moment. A few more tears rolled down her cheeks, but at least she didn't start sobbing. He kept wiping her tears away and when she finally opened her eyes again she gave him a small, sorrowful smile as thanks.

Nadzia went back to treating Xayvion's wound and asked, "What happened to you?"

"The shadows didn't only attack the castle, they attacked some parts of the city as well," he confirmed. "I was on the outskirts of Phexion on my way back here when they appeared."

"And you had to stay to protect the people," she added.

She didn't need to hear a reply, or see him nod, to know she was right. Xayvion would never leave the citizens of the kingdom unprotected.

"Are the civilians okay?"

"Yes, they are. A few were injured but nobody got killed thankfully."

"Good."

She bandaged up the cut and then got to her feet.

"Any other injury I should know about?" She asked. "You need to tell me about the small ones, too. We're about to go to war, you need to be in perfect shape."

He took his shirt off to reveal a few other cuts and scratches on his arms and abdomen. None of them were deep but they still needed treatment. She worked in comfortable silence, with Xayvion's eyes following her every movement.

"Had you been waiting outside for long?" He asked while he put his shirt back on.

"I needed to know if you were okay, but Kagen wouldn't let me go look for you, so I waited," she mumbled, looking embarrassed.

Xayvion looked glad to hear that Kagen had stopped her from leaving the castle to look for him.

"I should go see Lucjan now," he said.

She agreed, but instead of just letting him go, she walked with him to the meeting room. Now that she knew he was alright, she felt anxious about letting him out of her sight, as if looking away for a second would suddenly make her realise she'd imagined everything.

When they stopped in front of the door, he looked at her, a silent question in his eyes. As she didn't do or say anything, he asked, "Do you want to come in with me?"

"Can I?"

He nodded and she followed him inside. Lucjan was alone in the room and jumped to his feet as soon as he saw his friend.

"I sent men looking for you," he announced, trying to hide his worry.

"I'm alright, as you can see," Xayvion replied, giving him a small smile. "Nadzia's already treated my injuries."

At the mention of her name Lucjan seemed to finally realise the two of them weren't alone. His eyes softened a little when he looked at the anxious state she was still in.

"Thank you," Lucjan said warmly.

She replied with a nod.

"What do we do now?" Xayvion asked. "Do we have any information?"

"I sent Dacey to check out the situation. He should be back by dawn," Lucjan explained. "Everything is already in place. One word and we're ready to leave."

"Leave to go where?" Nadzia asked.

"As far away as possible from the civilians," he replied. "Somewhere we can fight without putting people in danger." He looked from Xayvion to Nadzia, then back to Xayvion. "You should rest now that you can. Soon we won't have enough time to do so. If we get word from Dacey before planned, I'll send someone to wake you up."

"I could use some sleep," Xayvion replied, his voice forcefully cheerful. He glanced at Nadzia while saying it and she knew he was trying to tell her she needed to rest as well.

"We should all rest," she agreed, saying goodbye for the night.

23.

A knock on the door awoke Nadzia, but she was sure she'd have woken up soon anyway because of the thumping migraine she'd had for hours.

She opened her eyes and realised the position she was in. Her head was laying on Xayvion's chest, his arm wrapped around her. He was breathing calmly and rhythmically, meaning he was still asleep. Nadzia did her best to move his arm without waking him up but wasn't successful. He groaned slightly and rubbed his eyes. She took the chance to move away and sit up, which woke him completely. He opened his eyes to glance in her direction.

"They've come to wake us up," she said, gesturing towards the door.

Xayvion, however, didn't seem to care about that.

"Did you manage to sleep?" He asked, looking serious.

She nodded. "Thanks to you."

Both of them had known she wouldn't have been able to rest, so when she'd surprisingly asked him to stay with her the night before, he'd agreed. He made her feel safe enough to fall asleep and she hadn't had a nightmare, either.

"Did you sleep well?" She asked, in return.

"Probably better than I have in a while," he replied, sitting up. "Pity we only had a few hours."

Nadzia hoped her unruly hair covered enough of her face because she was sure she was blushing. It was not the right time to think about the double meaning his words could have.

On the other side of the door, the person knocked again.

"We'll be out in a minute," Xayvion announced loudly.

Nadzia let him use her bathroom to wash and change quickly then, once he had left her room, she did the same. She met him outside her door and they walked to the meeting room together. The others were already there when they entered, with Kagen standing a little apart from the others, since he still wasn't completely comfortable around them without Nadzia present. He looked happy to see her, greeting her with a kind smile.

"I won't be wasting time with idle talk, because apparently we don't have much of it," Lucjan started, then he looked at Dacey and said, "Tell us what you saw."

Dacey nodded. "I saw an army of shadows and creatures halfway between here and Lake Naraka. They don't seem to be moving, for some reason it looks like they've just set up camp there." He frowned. Then, he added, "There were two men with them."

"What did they look like?" Lucjan asked.

"The taller one... had dark skin, long red hair and two small horns on his head."

"That should be Malkiya," Lucjan replied, lost in thought. "The horns must be one of the side effects of working with dark magic. What about the other guy?"

"I think he's some sort of demon, too. The color of his skin was slightly unnatural, almost grey, and had weird lines all over it that looked like veins, but they were a blueish white and almost seemed to glow. I've never seen anything like it."

"That's Cael," Nadzia said. "He's the hell hound. Malkiya's given him a human form."

"There was nothing human in the way he looked," Dacey mumbled. He looked scared almost.

Lucjan stepped in. "We don't know what they plan to do, whether they'll move and come to us or not. We need to go to them."

Faleece stepped forward to get everyone's attention. *'That might just be what he wants us to do'*, she signed.

"I know, but we can't risk them attacking the city and hurting the civilians," Lucjan replied.

Faleece knew that that was their only option, but still didn't look convinced.

"The soldiers are ready," Lucjan announced, "If none of you have a better idea, or something useful to say, we'll set off now."

He looked around at each one of them, but no one spoke.

"Alright, let's go."

Lucjan gave everyone a bit of time to put on their armour. The first layer of clothing was leather, then they had additional parts in metal to cover their arms and torsos. The soldiers carried these by hand, since they weren't comfortable to wear while traveling, and tied them to their horses. Nadzia was the only one without any armour, but Lucjan made sure to tell her

217

he would provide her with some later. Once everyone was ready, they grouped together outside the castle where their horses and cats were waiting for them along with the soldiers.

Kagen approached Nadzia.

"You should ride Jaya," he said, "so you can rest some more."

"I'm alright," she tried to say, but he wasn't having it.

"The journey will be long and I'm sure you didn't sleep much last night," he replied. "It'll be hard for you to relax on a horse. And you already know that Jaya can be quite a comfortable ride."

His eyes were kind but his expression told her that he wasn't taking a no for an answer. Nadzia thanked him and walked over to Jaya. While she was mounting the cat, she saw Kagen talking to Xayvion. She couldn't hear what they were saying or read their lips, but she saw Xayvion smiling at Kagen and giving him a pat on the back. Then they went to their horses.

When they started moving off, Nadzia was too tense and on edge to be able to lay down on Jaya like she had done a few days before. She tried to calm herself by playing with her fur, which Jaya didn't seem to mind.

People rushed to the streets to watch Lucjan and the army pass by. Everyone looked scared and Nadzia realised that those who hadn't been attacked by the shadows had heard stories from the others, or seen the injuries on their neighbors and friends. They didn't know what was going on, but they did know they were in danger. And they were afraid.

Nadzia found herself envying them for a second, for the fact that they would stay in the city and go on with their lives while they risked theirs to protect them. She immediately felt guilty and cursed at herself in her head. She was the one who had insisted on fighting with the other so she couldn't complain now, she had to see it through. After all, it was *her* fault that all of this was happening. Nadzia couldn't just watch without doing anything to change it.

There were now fewer houses along the road and Nadzia noticed something strange from afar. Only when they came closer did she see a group of soldiers with structures behind them— stone towers, fastened to carts led by horses. Nadzia had never written about movable towers in her story, indeed she hadn't even *thought* about them. But somehow she wasn't surprised that Lucjan had come up with new strategies by himself. He quickly gave the soldiers instructions and they joined the procession, bringing the towers with them.

The rhythm of the ride and her headache slowly led Nadzia to lay down on Jaya's back. When she opened her eyes again it was almost dark, and Kagen and Xayvion were riding next to her, one on either side.

"Are you feeling better?" Kagen asked.

"A little physically and emotionally numb," she replied, yawning. "But that nap was very much needed."

"Told you so," he said teasingly. She answered with a smile.

"We'll be stopping to rest soon," Xayvion stated. "Malkiya's camp is not too far from here, so we should rest and eat now, then attack tomorrow when we're at our best."

It felt weird to think of stopping now that they were so close to the actual start of it all, but it also made sense - they would need to recover their strength before they attacked. They had been traveling for hours nonstop, and most of the group was already sleep-deprived and injured from the previous night. In more ways than one, they were already at a disadvantage.

They stopped after sunset but didn't light any fires since they couldn't risk Malkiya noticing them, and ate their food cold. After dinner, they lay down in groups, with people taking watch to make sure everyone was safe.

Nadzia was alone with Xayvion and Kagen. They knew it would be difficult to fall asleep given the situation, so they sat together, set apart from the others, with Nadzia in the middle.

"We're really doing this, huh?" She said quietly. "We're going to war."

She noticed the two of them glance at each other with sorry looks.

"Unfortunately there's nothing encouraging I can say right now," Xayvion replied. "What we're about to do is neither pleasant nor satisfactory, no matter the outcome."

"I've only been around a few years longer than you, but I can confirm that it doesn't get better with time," Kagen added. "It's not going to be something you can easily forget, either."

She sighed and leaned her head on Kagen's shoulder. Out of the corner of her eyes she noticed Xayvion smiling softly at them. Her chest warmed, but she told herself not to let hope take control of her. They had other things to worry about.

They were silent for a bit while Nadzia thought of what to say.

"Whatever happens over the next few days, I want you to know that I'm glad I had the chance to experience this and that I got to meet you all," she started. "I'm especially grateful that I could meet you two. I never thought you would become so special to me."

They both took her hands in theirs and smiled.

"I'm glad too, that I could meet you," Xayvion replied.

"I'm glad that you decided to change the plot and come to the Elf Realm," Kagen added with a grin. "It was a weird meeting, but I can't deny I like the way things developed from there. You're both way more interesting and lovable than you imagine."

Seeing they were in the mood for confessions, Nadzia decided to take the chance to admit something to herself as well. Sitting there between Kagen and Xayvion, she felt the safest and happiest she'd ever been in her twenty-two years of life, and was terrified she could potentially lose it all.

NAME: Cael
HEIGHT: 180 cm / 5'11"
AGE: unknown
HAIR COLOR: black and white
EYE COLOR: blue
ENTITY: hell hound

24.

Nadzia's instincts were getting sharper. Or maybe she was already half awake because of her anxiety.

Her eyes snapped open and she sat up, looking around. The night was dark, but she could still see the figures of the soldiers sleeping and the ones that were on watch. Everything was silent apart from the quiet snores emanating from some of them.

She reached out to Kagen and Xayvion and shook them awake.

"Something's wrong," she whispered as they sat up.

They both frowned as they looked around, trying to understand what she meant. A moment later, they heard the first scream.

Everyone in the camp jumped to their feet, the first torches were lit and swords were unsheathed. With the light coming from the fires, they could make out the shadows flying towards them, rushing in through the trees.

Most of the shadows looked the same as the ones that had attacked them the other day— unidentified masses of darkness— but some were faceless black human silhouettes, also surrounded by black mist. The ones with seemingly human forms were holding long black swords.

Nadzia was so distracted by their arrival that she barely noticed Xayvion passing— or maybe more *throwing*— a sword at her. Next, he handed her a shield.

That had been the training she'd hated the most, and the one she wasn't good at. The fact that she was now armed for face to face combat didn't do her already racing heart any good at all.

A shadow appeared in front of them and Kagen sliced its talons with his sword, while Xayvion plunged his weapon into the darkness. The shadow screeched and disappeared. Nadzia was completely lost, so ended up following them into the fight. Shadows crept through the soldiers and cries of pain echoed around them, drowning out the sound of clashing metal. She tried to stay behind Kagen and Xayvion, hoping it would protect at least one side of her, while she fended off the shadows coming from other directions.

The first time Nadzia stabbed one of the shadows, she was taken back by the feeling. She'd imagined it would feel like slashing through air, maybe even thick air if that made any sense. She did not expect it to feel as if she were stabbing through flesh. She hesitated before attacking the second shadow, her hands trembling. But that wasn't the time to think about what felt wrong. It was either them or her, and she'd promised herself she would survive and go home.

She heard a loud neigh coming from her left and turned to see a horse laying not too far from her, panting and whimpering in pain, its side torn open, blood flowing out of it. She stepped back, her vision blurring for a second, head spinning at the disturbing sight. A hand on her back steadied her and Nadzia glanced behind her to meet Kagen's worried eyes. He didn't have time to ask her if she was alright or do anything else, as a new group of shadows was already rushing towards him.

Kagen and Xayvion fought their way through the darkness and Nadzia made sure she attacked any threat that came towards them from behind. Her mind was screaming with doubts and praise and scared propositions. She wasn't sure what was more chaotic: the battle around her, or the noise inside her head. It made it so much harder to focus on fighting.

One of the soldiers holding a torch stepped closer to her and Nadzia had a better vision of what was going on around her. She realised, to her surprise, that there weren't that many shadows compared to them, there only *seemed* to be more as it was night and everything around them was as black as the shadows themselves.

Nadzia was tired. Panting, she swung her sword at anything that moved. Some of the shadows pulled back with a strange hiss and ran towards other soldiers, while others were more insistent in their attacks.

"Fuck off already!" She cried out, frustratedly, slashing through a dark silhouette.

In time, the screeching seemed to die out, as did the sound of the swords. When at last she didn't have any more shadows in front of her, she let herself stop for a second and look around to assess the situation.

The creatures that had come for them were all dead. Or maybe it was better to say they had all been eliminated. Their status of living dead made things confusing.

Nadzia fell to her knees with a big sigh.

Despite this small victory, however, everyone around her seemed more worked up than during the fight. Soldiers were running around, looking for Lucjan and asking each other for instructions.

"Are you hurt?" Xayvion asked, rushing to crouch next to her. Kagen was standing behind him. Both of them looked at her worriedly.

"—'m okay," she blurted out, nodding more times than necessary.

"We have to go," Kagen announced.

They helped her up and she was surprised to find out her wobbly knees actually supported her weight again. She held back a burst of hysterical laughter.

Nadzia followed the two of them without really understanding where they were going, but when they stopped Lucjan was standing in front of them, busily giving his soldiers orders.

He looked at them. "He tried to ambush us, hoping to take us out while we were asleep. We can't wait anymore. We're moving and attacking now."

"But it's still night," Nadzia said helplessly.

Lucjan looked at her as if she were stupid, then seemed to realise who he had in front of him and blinked quickly, his expression becoming neutral again.

"If we wait, we could all be dead by sunrise," he explained. "We have to attack now, hoping to throw him off course."

Nadzia still didn't understand but was sure her brain was just being slower than usual to spite her. She pretended to know what he was saying and nodded to acknowledge his decision. He seemed to believe her.

Faleece ran to them and signed to Lucjan, '*We're ready to move, we're awaiting your order.*'

Lucjan looked back at Nadzia. "Go to one of the towers and find a place for yourself. We'll need you with our archers during the battle."

She felt slightly ashamed at the wave of relief that washed over her knowing she wouldn't be in the middle of the battle. She could still be in danger, but would surely be safer up there.

Lucjan then said to Faleece, "We'll set off as soon as she's settled."

Faleece nodded and walked off.

Kagen and Xayvion followed Nadzia as she went from tower to tower to find one that had a free space for her. Once she found the right one, she hesitated before she walked in.

"Be careful," she said to the two men standing in front of her. "Please be careful."

She was finally starting to understand her feelings for both of them and the thought she might lose them was devastating.

Kagen stepped forward first, pulling her to his chest.

"We'll be alright, don't worry about us," he whispered in her ear, giving her a long, tight hug then letting her go. A cold feeling enveloped her as soon as he stepped back.

Then it was Xayvion's turn. His eyes were so sad that Nadzia felt herself tearing up. He put a hand behind her neck and pulled her closer, kissing her forehead.

"Make us proud," he said quietly, with a small smile.

Nadzia clutched the fabric of her trousers, as she knew that if she didn't restrain herself she would grab both of them and never let them go. They watched her walk into the tower and she felt the first tear break free as soon as she closed the door behind her.

She took the stairs to the top of the tower. The other soldiers watched her walk to the only empty space without saying a word. She crouched down and left her shield and sword on the ground next to her. The woman beside her handed her a pile of leather clothes.

"Wear these," she said. "It's the only protection we have. Armour is too cumbersome for us."

Nadzia quietly thanked the woman and covered herself with the leather gear. As soon as she'd put the last piece on, the tower started moving. She leaned over to look at what was going on around them. Everyone was moving together as if they were part of one big machine. Nadzia wasn't sure if her thoughts made sense anymore but wasn't thinking clearly enough to judge.

The sound of paws and hooves, and the noise of the armour as they moved created something similar to a song. It was like one of those cinematic sounds aimed at building up tension before a major event. It shouldn't have been surprising, but still astonished her. Nadzia could feel the excitement building in her bones, in her heart hammering in her chest and in her ears.

She first tried to calm herself by numbering the soldiers, but lost count and restarted so many times that she decided to give up. Next, she tried to spot the people she knew in the crowd.

She saw Lucjan first. It was easy to find him, standing in front of everyone, leading the army, his armour shining in the moonlight.

Somewhere on the far left, she found Dacey's blond head. She could only see him from behind, but by the way he was sitting on his horse, he looked as if he hadn't suffered any injuries during the attack.

Almost directly in front of her, farther away from Lucjan than she had imagined would have been allowed, she could see Hedyah and Faleece, riding side by side. Her heart ached for them. They both cared a lot about their duty and the kingdom, but they also cared about each other. She didn't want to think about how hard it must be to fight alongside someone you love, knowing you might have to leave them to die to complete the mission.

Lastly, to Nadzia's right, close to her tower, she spotted Xayvion and Kagen. They, too, were riding side by side and seemed to be talking. It was a strange contrast to the silence and stoic expressions around them. She wondered what they were talking about.

She didn't like to think they were being separated. She didn't want to be alone.

The minutes dragged by and Nadzia noticed the scenery around them change. The trees disappeared to be replaced by dry fields.

When the tower stopped, Nadzia felt her heart stop as well. She closed her eyes, in denial.

No, she couldn't act like that. She needed to be strong. She needed to get through this to be able to go home.

She bit her lip and looked up.

In front of them, on the other side of the field, a massive shadow was waiting patiently for them.

25.

The first few rows of creatures she could see from the towers were shadows. Because of how dark they were, the mist surrounding their bodies and the fact that it was still night, Nadzia couldn't make out what the beasts behind them were.

In the middle of what she figured was the third row of shadows was Malkiya, standing tall in all his glory, dressed in black, looking like death incarnate. The wind was blowing through his long red hair, but he still looked perfectly neat. Cael, still in human form, was standing beside him.

Although he was still far away, Nadzia was sure she could see a grin on Malkiya's face.

She noticed Lucjan giving orders to the army, then riding forward on his horse. Nadzia came out in goosebumps at the thought of him walking towards the enemy alone. Sure, he was probably more powerful than his whole army put together, but it could still be dangerous. Malkiya used to be a god too after all, and they had no idea what he was capable of now.

Lucjan stopped in the empty space between the two armies.

"Malkiya, come forward," he ordered. His voice resounded throughout the whole field, reaching everyone's ears.

Malkiya just tilted his head, his grin growing wider, and ignored the order.

"You don't have to do this," Lucjan continued. "Whatever happened to you, whatever you need now, you can come to me and we can fix it together."

To everyone else it might have sounded like a reasonable last attempt at taking a peaceful route, but Nadzia could clearly hear the desperation in his voice. Lucjan did not want to fight Malkiya.

"We used to be friends," he added. "We still can be if you tell your army to retreat."

Nadzia felt her heart skip a beat when she saw Malkiya's grin disappear.

His expression completely neutral, he replied. "I want power, not friendship."

That must have been the signal, because as soon as he finished the sentence, the creatures around Malkiya started running towards Lucjan, whose army reacted quickly and rushed towards the enemy in return.

Chaos ensued, before Nadzia could even blink.

Shadows swept over the army and screams of pain and rage rang out, accompanied by the sound of metal against metal. The creatures clawed over the soldiers blocking their path and the elves' cats jumped in to do the same against the enemy.

Nadzia saw blood spray and a man's head being ripped off his shoulders, followed by high pitched laughter. The shadows seemed excited by the violence.

If Nadzia had thought the two previous battles she'd fought in were pandemonium, this one was pure, wicked, suicidal havoc. When she thought things were bad enough and couldn't take a turn for the worst, she saw them.

Dragons.

Well, they didn't really look like the dragons you usually see in movies and cartoons. They were more like giant lizards, or better, like komodo dragons, but with spiked tails, like the Kentrosaurus she'd once seen in a museum. A truly horrible mix.

How had she forgotten about them? She'd created them for fun but never used them in the story. Many of the things she had planned but never used had already showed up in the new plot, so *why* did she not think about *them*?

Nadzia remembered watching a documentary about komodo dragons with her father when she was little. Their size and ferocity had fascinated her so much she'd kept them in a little box somewhere in her brain. This had turned out to be useful when she was in need of a magical animal to create. Now, with these creatures in front of her, however, she was no longer fascinated.

She tried to remember what komodo dragons were like. They have a venomous bite, can grow to be ten foot long and kill and eat a human as if they were a mere rabbit. Komodo dragons were already deadly enough without the extra weapons on their tails. Nadzia did not want to find out how those ten foot long reptiles with spiked tails would tear them apart.

Why, why, why, why had she made them?

Nadzia was finally roused from her frozen state when the soldier next to her gave her a push, glaring at her.

"Get the fuck to work," she yelled.

Nadzia knew what to do.

They had elves on their side and big cats like Jaya, but those dragons would be a problem for everyone. It was up to the archers to take down as many of them as they could, before they massacred their soldiers and animals.

So she set to work, picking up her bow and shooting arrow after arrow.

Being the creator of those animals, Nadzia knew they weren't simple magical creatures. They didn't live in that world, but came from the underworld. They were creatures that Malkiya had brought back with him from the other side, which made them demons in animal form. This meant the new weapons mixed with gold would work on them as well— they simply had to get to the dragons before the dragons got to them.

The dragon's skin was very thick and not all the arrows penetrated it, but bounced off it instead. So the archers opted to go for their eyes. Definitely a harder target to hit, but Nadzia was pleased to realise that all the archers had unfaltering aim and perfect sight.

When her first arrow hit a dragon in the eye, the sound of pain coming from it made her shiver to the bone. It squirmed in agony for a few seconds before it stopped moving.

The yellowish-green field was quickly becoming red, with hints of a darker colored liquid. The air smelled of copper and acid, making Nadzia's stomach turn. She tried not to pay attention to the screams of pain coming from the soldiers, or the sound of the dragons' spikes stabbing them. She was sure she could hear bones breaking.

Nadzia finished the arrows in the quiver by her side, and someone rushed to replace them with new ones. Seconds, or maybe minutes, or maybe hours dragged by. Nadzia couldn't tell if time was slowing down or speeding up. It simply didn't seem real in that moment of chaos. Maybe they were stuck in the same moment that kept repeating itself.

At some point Nadzia's curiosity got the better of her. She stopped and allowed herself a moment of distraction.

She looked towards the other side of the field. All the shadows and dragons were fighting against them, so Malkiya was now standing on his side of the land completely exposed. Cael was back in his hound form, a dark mist dancing around his paws.

She knew it was a bad idea, but her brain couldn't come up with anything better. He was right there, and no one was trying to get to him, so she had to try it herself. He was very far away, but she knew she could reach him anyway. She pointed the arrow and shot.

She clearly saw Malkiya's hand come up and stop the arrow mid-air right in front of his face. He looked totally calm. *Way too calm*. He turned the arrow around and pulled his arm back, then threw it back in the same direction from which it had come.

Nadzia had no idea where she'd suddenly got those reflexes, but dodged the arrow just in time. The archer on the other side of her tower wasn't quite as lucky. No one stopped to see what had happened, or to make sure the person was still alive.

When Nadzia turned around again, Malkiya was still standing on his own, but his faithful Cael was no longer next to him.

26.

The hell hound was a flash of darkness running towards their army. He dashed through every opening he found, then jumped at any cat that tried to get in his way, his fangs sinking into their necks. The elves riding the unfortunate cats all tried to stab him while he was busy killing their animals, but although their swords cut into his flesh, Cael didn't seem to feel them. Only a little trail of blood escaped the cut before the wound healed. The riders were the next ones he attacked.

Nadzia froze. What was she supposed to do? What were any of them supposed to do? The shadows were mixed in with the darkness of the night and she could barely make out their numbers. The dragons were an issue that no one had expected. Cael was more powerful than the other creatures and he was out for blood. Nadzia wasn't even sure if Cael could heal himself or if his special connection with Malkiya did that.

Were they all going to die?

Nadzia punched herself in the leg to bring herself back to reality. She couldn't panic now. If she did, she would die. If she did, the people she cared about would die.

That thought suddenly reminded her that she hadn't seen any familiar faces since the fight had started. She picked up another arrow and scanned the battlefield, shooting dragons and shadows while searching for her friends.

Kagen was ferociously striking anything that crossed his path, his sword shining brightly in the moonlight. Jaya was doing the same, clawing and biting her way through the enemy. Both of them seemed to be alright. Maybe a little tired, but not injured. Nadzia shot an arrow into a dragon's eye just as it was preparing to attack Jaya from behind and Kagen cut its head off.

The weight on Nadzia's chest suffocated her more and more as she searched for Xayvion without success. Just as she was starting to panic, she caught a flash of metal on her right and knew before she looked that it was him. She saw him leap off his injured horse and land on a dragon's back. He swung his sword and cut its tail off near the body, then jumped off and cut its head, too. She watched him whirl away and fight with the shadows as if he were dancing. There was grace in the way he moved which contrasted weirdly with the fact he was killing. Nadzia helped him out as much as she could while he parred blades with a human shaped shadow and then dug his sword into it, making it disappear.

The tower shaking made Nadzia miss her next shot. She and the archers around her leaned forward to understand what the problem was. They saw a group of dragons hitting the stone with their tails and did their best to shoot them, but the angle wasn't right and there were too many to attack.

Pieces of the structure started to fall away and Nadzia realised her comrades were tying on their quivers and putting their bows on their backs. Her head jerked up, heart pounding, as she watched them pick up swords and run down the stairs. If she wanted to live, she had to get out of the tower as well. But there were dragons outside. There were shadows. There was Cael.

The tower shook again, which was enough to make her change her mind and convince her to follow the other soldiers. Nadzia put bows and arrows on her back and picked up her sword and shield, then fled down the stairs. The tower started to collapse as soon as she'd got out of it and she moved just in time before a huge piece of stone landed next to her, making her shriek in surprise.

Catching sight of the dragons out of the corner of her eye, she turned and hurried away. Nadzia wasn't proud of the fact that instead of fighting, she mostly ran around, but the sight of the dragons terrified her. She wasn't a fighter. She was pretending to be one because of the circumstances in which she found herself, but her fear of dying was stronger than her will. The shadows were nothing compared to dragons. The shadows were easy to kill in comparison. The dragons could stab you with their spikes or bite you so quickly you'd feel the pain even before you saw them move.

Nadzia ran towards the mass of darkness, as far away from the dragons as she could. The shield felt unbearably heavy and she silently thanked her adrenaline for providing her with enough strength to continue fighting. She closed the distance between herself and a group of black mist banks and dove right into it, slashing around, first blindly and then more carefully once she'd got the hang of it. The screeches around her were affecting her mind, which made her feel more unhinged and violent as a result.

Nadzia heard the sound of a skull shattering and turned to see a dragon inching towards her. She knew how fast it could be, so running wouldn't save her. It was taking its time to savor the moment before it caught its prey.

When the dragon shot forward, she saw a flash of brown and black jump onto it. Recognising it as Jaya, the fear of her getting hurt was so much greater than Nadzia's fear for her own life that she rushed towards her. Jaya was biting the dragon's body and probably waiting for the poison to take effect, but the dragon didn't want to go down so easily and it swung its tail at her. The spikes barely even scratched her before the dragon's tail fell to the ground, away from its body. Nadzia hadn't even realised that she had been the one to cut it.

Jaya left the body and approached Nadzia, to make sure she was okay. Nadzia looked around, but couldn't see any sign of Kagen. What if their getting separated meant he was injured, or worse?

"Where's Kagen?" She asked, freaking out. "Is he alright?"

She could swear she saw Jaya nod at her and she let out a short breath of relief.

Another wave of shadows ran toward them and they fought them together. Nadzia was extremely glad that Jaya didn't seem to want to leave her side. She could keep an eye on her and make sure she didn't get injured, and in return Jaya would do the same for her.

Nadzia halted for a second as an idea struck her. She wasn't sure why she hadn't thought of it sooner.

She turned to Jaya and yelled over the chaos, "We need to find Lucjan!"

The cat leaned down to make it easier for Nadzia to mount her. She sheathed her sword with trembling hands and picked up her bow again. Even if they were moving, Nadzia was sure she would be more useful shooting arrows than trying to stab anyone that passed next to them.

She trusted Jaya to take her to Lucjan while she focused on killing the enemies around them, especially the ones blocking their path.

Jaya destroyed the shadow Lucjan was fighting with one movement and he turned to them, taken aback.

"What the hell are you doing here?" He yelled, confused by Nadzia's presence. "You're supposed to be on the tower!"

"The tower collapsed," Nadzia announced briefly. "Listen, Malkiya has had to connect himself with the creatures and demons he brought back. This makes him more vulnerable, so the more creatures we kill the weaker he gets." She was aware that the number of creatures in his army was terribly high, probably higher than the number of soldiers they had. She was sure Lucjan was about to point that out when she added, "it should work the other way around, too. Since they're connected, if we bring down Malkiya, the rest of the creatures should die as well, or at least get significantly weaker."

He seemed to like that possibility.

"Are you sure about that?"

"I'm not sure about anything at this stage, but it *could* work," she replied. "He must be keeping his distance for a reason."

Lucjan looked behind her and she noticed his stare harden at the sight of his old friend.

"It's worth a shot," he said.

Taking one step forward, he looked back at her.

"If you see me struggling call for backup," he said. "Hedyah, Faleece, or Xayvion if you can."

She nodded, then said. "Be careful."

He gave her one long, sad look.

"You too," he replied, then ran past them towards Malkiya.

27.

Nadzia needed to keep an eye on Lucjan to understand when he needed help, but hadn't realised how hard it would be to watch him and fight for her own life at the same time. She had been watching other people fight for the whole duration of the battle, so why was it suddenly so hard to do? Jaya protecting her made it a little easier, but she suddenly found it hard to focus on both things. It was as if the shadows had decided to keep her busy at a time when what she actually needed were fewer distractions.

She saw Lucjan run towards Malkiya and hoped Cael was too busy fighting to notice that his master was about to be attacked. Malkiya didn't seem scared or troubled by the sight of his former friend running towards him, armour shining and sword ready to strike.

When they were in the upper realms together, they'd always fought side by side. While Lucjan's duty had been to protect people during wars, Malkiya was the true war god, the one whose duty it was to kill and wreak havoc.

When Lucjan was close enough to attack and struck the first time, Malkiya simply dodged his attempt, as unbothered as he had been when he'd stopped Nadzia's arrow earlier on.

She tore her eyes away from them when she was pushed down by one of the human shaped shadows. It brought its sword down to stab her but she covered herself with her shield. Before it could react, her foot came up and kicked it in the face, then she moved her sword up, digging it into the shadow's chest. There was a screech before it disappeared into mist.

Getting back up onto her feet Nadzia noticed Hedyah fighting a few feet away from her. Despite the dark blood covering her, she didn't look tired, nor injured, but on good form. She was almost shining.

Nadzia heard a loud noise coming from her left and turned quickly, ready to help, thinking Jaya was in danger. But it wasn't Jaya who needed help.

Faleece had fallen, spitting blood on the ground. Part of her armour was on the ground and from the way she was holding herself Nadzia knew she was injured. In front of her there was a dragon, clearly intent on finishing her off. A couple of shadows floated around behind it, their high pitched laughter filling the air.

"Jaya!" She yelled.

The cat turned towards her and Nadzia pointed at Faleece. Jaya didn't need any further instructions and quickly headed to her aid. Nadzia ran in the opposite direction.

She fought her way to Hedyah, who looked surprised when she saw Nadzia next to her.

"Faleece is injured," Nadzia announced, cutting a shadow in two.

She felt Hedyah stiffen next to her.

"She's more important than whatever mission we have at the moment," she continued. "You need to fight by her side."

"The shadows…" Hedyah started, voice rough.

"Lucjan himself is taking care of Malkiya," Nadzia explained. "If he manages to bring him down, all these creatures may cease to function. I'll get Xayvion and Kagen and we'll go help him. You need to get to your girlfriend before it's too late."

After a heartbeat of silence, Hedyah asked, "Where is she?"

Nadzia pointed in the direction of Faleece and Hedyah started running towards her without hesitation. Both the dragon and the two shadows had been killed, but Faleece was now holding her side and leaning on Jaya for support.

Nadzia cut a dragon's tail while it was attacking another soldier, and they finished it off by cutting off its head. When she turned around again Jaya was rushing towards her.

Nadzia mounted her, "Let's find Kagen."

She switched weapons again while Jaya confidently headed in a specific direction. Maybe she had a special connection to Kagen that told her where he was all the time. That would be something she'd have to remind herself to ask him once the battle was over.

Kagen flashed a big smile when he saw them arrive.

"You're keeping yourself busy, I see," he teased, while casually stabbing a shadow.

"Get on, we need to find Xayvion," Nadzia said.

Her serious, rushed tone made his smile disappear. He jumped onto Jaya and sat behind Nadzia.

"He was further down towards the right end of the field last time I saw him," he said pointing out the direction. Jaya jumped into action again.

The night sky was turning lighter, the sun was beginning to rise, bringing light onto the battlefield and making it easier to see the enemy.

Nadzia felt Kagen put his hand on her waist and squeeze it gently.

"You're doing great," he whispered in her ear. "Just hang on a little longer."

She covered his hand with hers, relishing the comfort of his touch. Nadzia had to let go, albeit reluctantly, when she finally noticed Xayvion from afar and realised he was fighting more creatures than one person could possibly take down on their own. She grabbed an arrow and started shooting the shadows he couldn't deal with. Noticing the sudden disappearance of the enemies that had been in front of him just a second before, he turned around and saw his friends. The surprised pleasure in his eyes turned to worry a second later.

"What's going on?"

"Get on," she ordered, "we need to help Lucjan."

Xayvion didn't need to be told twice. He mounted as well, sitting behind Kagen. Nadzia was grateful Jaya was big and strong enough to bear so much weight.

While they charged towards Lucjan, she noticed Cael on the other side of the field, running parallel to them.

"Lucjan is fighting Malkiya on his own," she yelled so that both of them could hear her. She pointed at the hell hound. "We need to make sure Cael doesn't get between them!"

Kagen leaned down and patted Jaya's side. "Baby I know it's a lot to ask of you, but you need to pick up your pace," she told her. "We've got to get there before the hound does."

With a growl, Jaya forced herself to run faster. The three of them readied themselves, weapons in hand. Cael was unnaturally fast, and Jaya barely had any advantage on him. Nadzia pointed her arrow and shot. It only grazed Cael's snout and landed in front of him, but that was enough to stop him and bring the focus of his attention onto them.

"I'm starting to regret this," Nadzia mumbled.

The three of them jumped off Jaya as Cael launched himself towards them.

When Kagen and Xayvion both stepped forward to stand in front of Nadzia, she wasn't sure what feeling washed over her first: worry that they would get hurt trying to keep her safe, or relief that she wouldn't be the first one the hell hound got to.

The situation exploded so quickly that she could barely keep track of what was happening. Cael was fast in his movements, but both Kagen and Xayvion had unnatural speed in their skillset, too. Cael's angry growl made the earth under their feet shake. Nadzia saw flashes of claws and swords colliding with each other. Jaya tried to jump in as much as she could, but Kagen and Xayvion were making it hard for her to find an opening.

The hell hound made eye contact with Nadzia and finally seemed to realise that the two men were trying to fight him while keeping him away from her. He growled once more and shouldered his way between them, knocking them both to the ground. He swung his claws at her and, despite her attempt at moving away, she wasn't fast enough. Jaya jumped and dug her fangs into Cael, both of them tumbling away from Nadzia.

Nadzia looked down at her left shoulder, where two big gashes were now staining her clothes and leather in blood. She swallowed the lump in her throat and bit her lip so as not to cry out in pain.

She hadn't even realised Kagen was standing in front of her until she heard him curse under his breath.

"It's fine, it's fine, it's not deep." He sounded like he was trying to convince himself more than her.

She glanced behind Kagen and saw Xayvion fending off Cael with Jaya at his side. Kagen's head blocked her vision again and she realised he had cut a piece of fabric from his shirt and was trying to tie it around her shoulder to stop the bleeding.

When she'd thought up her plan, Nadzia had intended to get rid of Cael so that Lucjan could fight Malkiya without getting disturbed, but she wasn't so sure that he could be killed anymore. Cael was tougher than he looked. At this point, they were only trying to buy Lucjan time.

A scream of pain to her right made them all stop and turn. Malkiya was holding his shoulder, black blood flowing out of a wound. His neutral expression had been replaced with one of anger. Nadzia noticed the veins around his neck turning dark.

Cael limped forward, and that's when Nadzia realised something: Cael and Malkiya were more closely connected than she'd originally imagined. It wasn't possible he would react like that just from a blow from Lucjan. The thing on his neck must have been a reaction to Jaya's poison, the poison she'd injected when she'd bitten Cael just a few moments earlier. Malkiya and Cael shared injuries and the bond seemed to go both ways.

Nadzia's body reacted before her mind did. She leaned down and picked a dagger up off the ground that had probably been dropped by a soldier during the fight. She had never thrown a knife or a dagger in her whole life, and she hadn't tried during her training with Xayvion either, but at that moment it didn't matter. When she saw Cael turn his back to them to run to his master's aid, she threw the dagger with as much strength as she could muster, copying the movement she had seen many times in movies.

The dagger sank into Cael's neck and he emitted a rasping noise in response.

In the same split second, Xayvion jumped onto Cael to dig his sword into his side, and Lucjan stepped forward to dig his into Malkiya's.

Maybe it was the fact that they were both attacked at the same time, or that they were already sharing each other's injuries along with the ones from the creatures in their army, but Cael and Malkiya stopped moving, their mouths open in silent screams. When Xayvion and Lucjan pulled back their swords, the hound and his master started convulsing and then a second later their bodies melted into a dark puddle on the ground.

The five of them stared, momentarily in shock. Even Jaya looked confused by what had just happened.

Lucjan was the first to move. He leaned down to touch the puddle, seeming to analyze it, as if its entity could make any sense or explain the fact that it had been a living being just a moment before. Then he stood up again and turned to them.

He looked behind them, to the army and the fight, and his eyes widened in surprise.

At that, Nadzia turned as well, Xayvion and Kagen stepping forward next to her.

The shadows were all turning into mist and disappearing, leaving the soldiers surprised and confused, their swords half raised. Only the dragons seemed to be alive, but the way they moved was clearly clumsier and not many of them were left anyway. With the soldiers rushing to take care of them, it wouldn't be long before all the enemies were finally gone.

"It actually worked."

Nadzia jumped at the voice, not expecting to find Lucjan next to her. He smiled down at her, relieved.

"I'm surprised, too," she replied, with an anxious chuckle.

She couldn't believe her theory was real and that her plan had actually worked.

Momentarily they had let their guard down. They were too busy watching the battlefield and breathing in relief at the fact that everything was almost over that none of them noticed the dragon creeping up behind their group.

There was a sound of bones breaking and flesh being ripped open— everyone turned. Everyone but Nadzia.

She looked down, gasping for air. Two long, bloody spikes were coming out of her stomach. The sight troubled her more than the burning feeling that was beginning to take over her body.

She heard movements around her and saw the spikes disappear, but didn't really register what was going on. She put a trembling hand onto her stomach and it shocked her to see it was covered in blood. She bit back a sorrowful laugh. All that effort and training, and she was still going to die.

Xayvion's arms caught her as she fell.

She watched him panic, eyes quickly dancing all over her body without actually seeing her, cradling her head in his arms.

"No, no, no," he whispered, in denial.

She didn't have the strength to turn her head away, so she was stuck watching Xayvion fall apart. It was the worst sight she could have witnessed. She felt hot pain all over her body, a taste of blood in her mouth, and it was difficult to breathe. Despite this, she tried to calm him down, as the look in his eyes hurt more than her wounds.

"It's okay," she weakly said. "I'm okay."

His head snapped up, looking at the people around them, looking for something, or someone.

"Do something!" He yelled.

"I can't," she heard Kagen reply, his voice shaking. "I can't heal her."

Kagen's strained voice told Nadzia he was about to break down as well, just as Xayvion was. Thinking of both of them falling apart in front of her, because of her, broke her heart.

"It's okay," Nadzia repeated, her voice ragged.

This time Xayvion really looked at her.

"I'm sorry," he cried, tears flowing down his cheeks. His shaking hand gently brushed her hair out of her face. "I broke my promise. I'm sorry."

She wasn't sure if the tears on her face were hers or just his.

"It's okay." She kept repeating it over and over. She wanted to tell him it wasn't his fault. She wanted to tell him not to cry for her.

Kagen— who she hadn't realised was kneeling next to her now— pressed something onto her wound but it wasn't enough. It was already too late and she had already lost too much blood.

"Our time was borrowed anyway..." she whispered, a tiny smile appearing on her lips. Even if they weren't meant to last, at least she would be leaving with fond memories of them. It was enough for her.

Xayvion's usually warm eyes were clouded with tears and panic. Her heart broke for him. She tried to bring her hand up to wipe his tears away but couldn't move. Her limbs were too heavy.

Nadzia briefly looked beyond them, at the crimson sunrise. The color made Nadzia think of a phoenix flying in the small space between their heads. Phoenixes were signs of hope and rebirth, so she chose to consider that a good sign.

Nadzia moved her eyes one last time, focusing on Kagen. He, too, was crying. She felt so guilty knowing she was the reason they were both hurting. She gave him a small smile to comfort him because talking was suddenly impossible.

Kagen leaned down and pressed a kiss on her forehead. He whispered, his voice shaking but still incredibly soft, "You are loved and we are proud of you," knowing it would be the last thing she heard.

The hot pain started to be replaced by cold.

She was already half gone when she closed her eyes, but she could swear she heard someone scream in sorrow.

28.

Nadzia stretched in bed, content with how soft it felt. She hugged her pillow as she slowly woke up. For the first time in a long while, she felt as if she had had a good night's sleep.

Her eyes opened and the first thing she saw was the clock on her nightstand, telling her it was past noon. She shot up, panicking. Was she late for work? When she picked up her phone to check for missed calls from her boss, she read the date and realised it was a Sunday, so fell back on her bed in relief.

She felt unusually inspired. Realising she didn't want to spend the rest of her day in bed like she usually did, she got up and headed to the bathroom to take a shower and get ready to go out.

Something in the back of her head started bothering her. It felt weird, but she couldn't explain what it was. She brushed it away. Maybe she just wasn't used to sleeping so well.

It was when she went to take her shirt off, that she noticed something weird. On her left shoulder there were two long scars that looked as if they had been caused by animal claws. She stared at herself in the mirror, eyebrows furrowed. Her eyes went lower till they stopped at her stomach. There, another two scars marked her. She ran her fingers over them, confused. What were they doing there? How had she gotten them?

She was still touching the scars when images started shooting through her mind, like a movie being played in fast-motion. She saw shadows, soldiers dropping to the ground, big cats with massive fangs running among the corpses, dragons with spiked tails. She saw Kagen and Xayvion.

She put her shirt back on and ran back to her room, straight to her desk. She picked up the manuscript laying on it, opened it, and started reading.

That wasn't the story she'd written. It wasn't the same manuscript she'd given her best friend to read.

It was the story she'd actually lived in, the world she'd experienced. She was in it, as one of the characters.

"It was real…" she whispered, shocked.

She turned the pages until she reached the last one, sitting down to read it.

The Phexion army gathered the fallen and injured and made its way home. Xayvion and Kagen rode either side of the carriage that carried Nadzia's body. The ache in their hearts was so great that everyone around them could feel their sorrow.

Lucjan held a grand funeral for all the fallen soldiers, humans, valkyries and elves alike, and the whole kingdom mourned them.

For Nadzia, they held a private funeral. They met with her one by one.

Kagen sat beside her body for hours, staring at her in disbelief. He'd imagined they'd have had more time to get to know each other properly. He'd dreamt of her returning to the Elf Realm with him, of holding her and Xayvion in his arms, at a time when there was no war and no enemies. He couldn't believe he'd let that future slip through his fingers like this.

Xayvion entered the room after him. He held Nadzia's cold hand in his. He cried and apologized over and over again. The promise he'd made her replayed in his head like a broken record, mocking him for failing in the only thing he'd sworn to do, for failing her.

The rest of the group also visited her corpse, each of them thanking her for the help she'd offered them and apologizing for the wrongs they committed.

After the period of mourning, Lucjan buried Nadzia in the royal burial area in the castle.

No, that couldn't be it. She couldn't leave them like that, it wasn't fair.

They needed to know she was alright. She had to tell them.

That's when she realised the next two pages were blank. She was aware that she might have been making up weird theories out of panic and despair, but it wouldn't hurt to try. She picked up her pen and started writing. After a few sentences, the world around her blurred.

She found herself in Lucjan's meeting room. The whole place blurred, disappeared and then reappeared around her a few times before it stabilized. Lucjan and Dacey were standing in front of her, staring at her in shock. A moment later Dacey ran out of the room, yelling.

"It worked," she whispered, chuckling nervously, looking at Lucjan who was staring at her with wide eyes, still in silence.

The door was thrown open and Dacey ran back in, with Hedyah, Faleece and Xayvion right behind him.

"Hi," Nadzia said, taken aback.

"Please tell me I'm not imagining this," Xayvion begged, his voice shaking.

She gave him a sad smile and shook her head. "I'm real."

He ran towards her, ready to envelop her in his arms, but instead passed right through her body. They both tensed, equally surprised.

"What's going on?" He asked, trying to touch her again unsuccessfully.

"I guess I'm not really here," she realised sadly. Xayvion's hand stopped mid-air, his eyes widening with the realization that he really couldn't touch her.

"Would you mind telling us what's going on?" Lucjan asked, confused. His voice was strained when he added softly, "We buried you."

She had rushed back into this world without thinking about what to do or say. It would be hard to explain now, when she hadn't even processed it herself yet. Everyone's eyes were on her and she was surprised to realise they looked sad.

"I did die in this world," she clarified. "But I woke up back in mine."

"You went home," Xayvion whispered. His voice was so full of relief, Nadzia felt herself tear up. Phexion had become her home too in a way, but she couldn't tell them. If she did, it would only make this goodbye harder.

"I thought this was all a dream at first, but I have the scars," she continued, bringing a hand to her stomach. "My manuscript has changed, too. It now tells the story of what happened since I joined your world." She chuckled sadly. "I'm one of my characters now."

"I'm glad to know you're alright in your world," Dacey stepped in. He looked like he wanted to reach out and hug her. "We were all devastated after what happened."

The group slowly shifted closer, surrounding her. She looked around, at every single one of them. "Thank you for taking care of me. In life, and in death."

"I'm sorry we couldn't do more," Lucjan replied. He looked guilty and Nadzia couldn't help wondering if he blamed himself for her death.

"You did everything you could," she reassured him. Lucjan gave her a tight lipped smile in reply. "I'm really glad I got to meet you. Despite everything, I loved every single moment I spent in this world."

Hedyah stepped forward, catching Nadzia's attention. Only then did Nadzia realise that she and Faleece had openly been holding hands.

"I never got the chance to thank you for telling me about Faleece that day," she said. "So thank you. Very much."

Nadzia smiled in reply.

'*You saved my life*,' Faleece signed. '*If you hadn't warned Hedyah I would be dead now. Thank you*'

"You're welcome," Nadzia replied sincerely. She was glad she'd managed to help someone.

She then turned to face Xayvion. He looked away, ashamed.

"It wasn't your fault," she told him, softly. "I don't blame you for what happened so don't you dare blame yourself." He looked as if he wanted to disagree, but she cut him off. "I'm grateful for everything you did for me and for the moments we shared. You saved me in more ways than you could ever imagine."

"But I couldn't save you when it mattered," he replied, making her heart ache.

"I'm not dead. I'm just not part of your world anymore," she said. Her own statement, however, just made everything worse. "But I guess it's kind of the same thing."

"I wish I could hold you," he whispered. She could see him clenching his fists, holding himself back from trying to touch her again.

Frustrated for not being able to reach out to him, a tear rolled down her cheek. "I know. I'd like to do that, too."

"Will you be able to come back again?" Dacey asked hopefully, changing her focus.

"I'm not sure. There were only a few pages left in the manuscript and I used them to come here now," she answered. She saw Dacey's hope die. "I don't know if it only works if I write on the manuscript, or if I can come back into the story by writing wherever. But quite honestly, I'd rather think it won't be possible to come back at all, than hope for something that might never happen."

"So this is a goodbye," Lucjan added.

She nodded. There were a few moments of silence, then Nadzia tried to pull herself together. She looked around the room one last time.

"What about Kagen?" She asked, hesitantly.

"He went back to the Elf Realm," Xayvion explained.

Her heart broke a little bit more. She'd come back to let them know she was okay and to tell the men she had begun to love not to be sad. Why couldn't she have appeared at a time when they were both present?

She took a deep breath to force herself to hold back her tears.

"Please tell Kagen that I'm sorry I couldn't say goodbye to him," she told Xayvion, her voice breaking. "Tell him I—"

The world around her blurred and the next time she blinked she was sitting at her desk in her bedroom.

"No, no, no, no…."

She panicked, flipping the pages of the manuscript but there was no space left for her to write.

Her hand slammed over her mouth but it wasn't enough to stop her from breaking down.

That can't be the end.

There was so much she still had to tell them.

She picked her pen up again and wrote between the lines and on every inch of space she could find.

Nothing happened.

She turned the paper around and wrote in the margins, in every direction possible.

Nothing happened.

She took random papers, and post-it notes and notebooks and wrote, wrote, wrote and wrote.

Nothing changed.

She wrote, wrote and wrote, but she never moved from her bedroom.

EXTRA

CONTENT:

The following chapters contain scenes told from other character's point of view as well as extra moments.

1.

THE FIRST MEETING

DACEY

The peace and order in the kingdom were about to be broken, again.

Many families had sent in reports that strange creatures had been roaming around the fields in previous weeks. No one was ever able to describe the beasts for some reason, but all the civilians who claimed to have seen them kept mentioning how threatening their auras were. There was no real proof of the existence of these creatures at first, since other than the supposed sightings, the animals hadn't attacked or done anything to hurt anyone.

That was true until a week ago, when King Lucjan received an alarming report. Creatures had attacked some of the villages in the north-west part of the kingdom, near Lake Naraka. Lucjan sent Hedyah and Faleece, together with a group of soldiers, to assist the villages and learn more about what had happened. He had looked troubled by the problem, as if caught by something he hadn't expected, which worried Dacey a little.

The villages on the east had not been attacked, but they had also reported sightings, so in order to make sure they were safe— and to prevent other unpleasant surprises— Lucjan had sent Xayvion and Dacey to check on them.

They had gone from village to village asking people about the sightings, both as soldiers of Phexion, and undercover. Usually it was Dacey who went undercover. He had fun changing his appearance and walking into pubs or shops to listen to the latest gossip about the creature who allegedly roamed the fields and farms.

When they arrived at the last village of their tour, Xayvion went around with the soldiers to ask about the creature officially, while Dacey headed into a tavern to do his job in his own way. This time, he decided to keep his true appearance. They were far enough away from Phexion, and the villages before this one had only ever seen his other faces, so there was no risk using his real face there.

The owner of the Golden Fields pub had been useful to Lucjan in the past so they had kept the place as a meeting point, instructing the workers to comply with everything Dacey said after he showed them his royal ring, even if they didn't recognize his face. Dacey found it amusing that the staff had no idea that it was always he who went there, just wearing a different disguise.

Dacey walked to the counter and sat on one of the few available stools. It was almost evening but the place was already crowded. He subtly showed the barkeeper the ring, who nodded in reply, then ordered a beer to blend in. Dacey spent the first few minutes listening to the conversations around him, trying to find out something that could be useful, or a conversation he could introduce himself into. Luckily for him the matter of the beast was still a popular topic.

"I told you I've seen it!" A man to Dacey's right told his friend. "You know it was real! Your wife said she saw it too!"

Dacey had no time to waste, so butted in.

"Are you talking about the creature?" He asked.

Both men turned to him. The first— the one who claimed to have seen it— was large with dark features and two day stubble. He looked pleased someone else had mentioned the matter.

"Yes! Have you seen it, too?"

"Actually no, but I'm very curious," Dacey replied. "I hear everyone talking about it, but can never discover what it looks like. You've seen it, you say?"

"Yes, I saw it for the first time a couple weeks ago and then again a few days ago."

Dacey saw his friend shaking his head in disappointment.

He pushed him a little. "What did it look like?"

The man halted, his cheeks flushing. "Well… actually… I don't really know."

Dacey frowned, confused. "What do you mean?"

"It only seems to appear when it's dark so it's always very hard to see what it looks like," the man explained. "But I noticed it because I suddenly felt like I was being watched even though there was no one around. Everything seemed darker than it usually is at night, but a few times I saw something bright blue in the darkness and I'm sure they were its eyes!"

"Has it ever shown itself to anyone else?"

His friend replied for him. "No, no one seems to have actually *seen* the creature, which is why many of us don't believe it's real," he then turned to his big friend and added, "and you only bring this up when you're drunk. Do you really want me to believe you're not making it up?"

Dacey tried to hold back a frustrated sigh. Would this information be useful, or reliable even?

"Does it just wander around?" He kept on asking questions. "Has it ever attacked anyone or stolen food?"

"No, nothing like that."

Thankfully they were too far away from Lake Naraka to know what had happened to the villages there, but it wasn't official that those attacks had been by this same creature. They would have to wait for Hedyah's report before drawing any conclusions.

Dacey tried to keep the conversation going and gather as much information as he could, even from other people around them who heard their conversation and wanted to give their opinion on the matter. Dacey was glad everyone was so willing to talk about the creature, but could feel that many of the things they said were exaggerated or not entirely true, which made his job so much harder.

When he finally felt he'd gathered enough information, Dacey paid the barman and made to walk out of the pub. On the other side of the room, a young woman had just walked in. Her curly brown hair was sticking to her face, which was flushed and had trails of sweat on it, and she was dressed in clothes he'd never seen before. She stopped in the middle of the room and was staring at him as if she'd seen a ghost. An alarm went off in Dacey's head.

At first he thought he'd imagined it when he heard her whisper his name, but the expression on her face made him realise she actually had. From the way she was looking at him it was clear she knew him. But that was impossible.

Dacey had no idea who she was, he was sure he'd never seen her before, but if she really knew who *he* was, then she could be dangerous. He took advantage of her moment of surprise to close the distance between them and grab her wrist. She followed him without fighting, which only confused Dacey more. He took her up to the first floor, where the owner had rooms reserved for when they came by, and pushed her inside one. He hit her on the back of the head, quickly grabbing her before she fell and carried her to a chair where he sat her down and proceeded to tie her up. Once she was settled and safely restrained, Dacey left the room. He went back to the ground floor and glanced around the room, looking for the other soldier who was also acting as a civilian. They locked eyes from afar and Dacey gestured for him to come over.

"Is it time to go?" The soldier asked.

Dacey nodded. "Find Xayvion. Tell him to prepare to leave and then come here. There's something he needs to see."

The soldier nodded and walked out, while Dacey went back to the room. He sat on the table in front of the girl and waited for her to wake up. She looked so out of place, and not only because of how she was dressed.

Dacey watched her closely as she started to regain consciousness. When her eyes opened fully she looked around and then down at her bindings, but for some reason she didn't look troubled. She actually seemed to accept her situation pretty quickly. Too quickly in fact.

"I'm going to ask you some questions, and you're going to answer me truthfully," Dacey started, hoping to intimidate and get some sort of a reaction out of her. "I think you can already predict what will happen if you don't."

"I'll die?" She asked. She looked as if she were holding back a grin.

Dacey was confused, but played along with her. "Good guess."

"And there I was hoping we were going to become friends."

She was starting to irritate him. Why was she so calm?

"Sarcasm won't get you anywhere," he replied. He stared deep into her eyes and started with the questions. "Who are you?"

Her reply was fast. "I'm no one."

He bit the inside of his cheek to keep calm. "I'll ask again," he said in a low voice, leaning towards her, "who are you?"

She half shrugged, a mockingly innocent look on her face. "I'm literally no one important. I'm not even supposed to exist in this world."

In a rush of anger, Dacey grabbed his sword and pointed it at her neck. If she wasn't going to cooperate, he needed to do something else. If she couldn't be intimidated by words, he would try with actions. She seemed taken back by his gesture.

His voice was low, but clearly irritated, when he said slowly, "You already know how this will end, and you still don't want to cooperate. Are you not afraid of death?"

Her whole expression changed. Her eyes saddened and her shoulders dropped. Even her tone changed, becoming quiet and serious.

"I'm terrified, actually," she replied.

He reminded himself to keep still and not move his sword or react at all. He wouldn't be swayed by a little sadness. It could easily just be a trick to get him to lower his guard.

"Let's try again," he said, deciding to ask the most important question, "how do you know me?"

She looked a little unsure when she replied, "I created you."

He thought he'd heard wrong at first. *She created him?* What was that even supposed to mean? Was she crazy? Was that the reason she was behaving like this?

A knock on the door dragged him away from his thoughts. He gave her a look as if to say *'We're not finished yet'* and walked out of the room, where Xayvion was waiting for him.

"What's going on?" He asked.

"There was a girl in the pub," Dacey started whispering, "She knows who I am, which is pretty much impossible, and she keeps saying weird things. Maybe she's crazy. I think we should let Lucjan deal with her."

Xayvion frowned. "Are you sure it's safe to take her to the city, and even more so, to the king?"

Dacey thought about it for a second. She might know dangerous and important information, such as his true identity, but she didn't seem sane enough to use it against them. He didn't think she would be a threat to them.

"She seems to be a regular human being. She could only do us harm if she managed to leave Phexion after meeting with the king, but that will probably never happen."

Lucjan would decide her fate, but she likely wouldn't be able to leave Phexion. If he deemed her an enemy, she would either be locked up for good or executed.

"Alright then, bring her downstairs." Xayvion replied. "The carriage is ready."

Dacey nodded and watched him walk away before he entered the room again. This young woman was bad news and he had a really unpleasant feeling about the whole situation.

2.

THE ELF REALM

XAYVION

While they walked through the Elf Realm, all Xayvion could think of was Nadzia's secret.

It was all he had been able to think about for a while, actually, ever since she'd accidentally let out that she knew sign language. It wasn't even a big deal, if he thought about it, but at the same time it felt like it was.

Nadzia said she had kept it a secret to protect herself, and he understood that deep down, but it still didn't feel right. She'd desperately been trying to tell them what she claimed to be the truth ever since they'd met, and the fact she'd withheld this little nugget of information felt like a betrayal. For all they knew, she could have used her knowledge of sign language to read their private, political conversations and report them to the enemies. Now that he thought about it, they still knew nothing about her. They had no information about her identity nor her real intentions. Maybe she was working with Malkiya. That would explain everything she knew about Lucjan and all the information about Malkiya himself. Maybe he had sent her to mislead them into destroying their own kingdom without him doing the work. Maybe going to the Elf Realm was a trap, and now it was already too late to go back.

He had been a fool to let himself be swayed. He'd kept focusing on her emotions at first, in case he felt something wrong that would give her away, and accidentally ended up feeling connected to her. Her feelings were so intense that it was often hard for Xayvion to detach himself from them.

If he wanted to make sure the kingdom, and Lucjan, were safe, Xayvion would have to distance himself from his and Nadzia's feelings. He had to stop believing everything she told them and keep his head clear. They had a plan, after all— one that he didn't fully accept, but that he had agreed to anyway.

The group followed the two elf soldiers into the mountain and along a corridor. They opened the door to a room and told the group to wait inside while they went to tell the king they were there. Once inside Xayvion turned around to ask something, but one of the elves cut him short before he could speak.

"You will meet the king when we say so," is what he said a moment before closing the door and locking them in the empty room.

Xayvion was taken aback for a second. He had to calm his own anxiety and tune out the momentary fear and confusion he felt from the others. He needed to keep a clear mind.

He turned to Faleece. "Would you be able to break down the door?"

'*I could try,*' she signed.

She moved towards him, but after one step Nadzia spoke up.

"Wait!" she said. She looked annoyed. "We're here to ask for help, we can't cause trouble."

"They've just locked us in here." Xayvion felt bad about the tone of voice he used to speak to her, but then reminded himself that she could very well be an enemy and that she didn't deserve kind treatment.

"Yes, I'm well aware of that," Nadzia replied drily. "But we need them and we can't mess this up no matter what. Waiting for them to let us out and take us to the king will still give us a chance. If you try to get out of here by force, you can say goodbye to that chance."

Seeing Nadzia upset and feeling her anger through his powers only made him more upset. Why was *she* angry at them? She was the one trying to make a fool out of them.

"We shouldn't do anything stupid," she said finally.

"She's right," Dacey agreed.

Xayvion didn't want to accept that. He didn't want to give her what she wanted. This could all have been part of her plan. She did, indeed, look calmer than she should.

Nadzia then added, "Settle down, we'll have to wait."

Xayvion looked at the others and could feel them accepting that they were just supposed to wait. Dacey was the first to go and sit down. Xayvion and Faleece did the same right after.

At first Xayvion tried his best to calm down and just wait, but *everything* was too loud. Both his mind and his heart were in chaos.

From time to time he glanced at Nadzia. She was asleep, and he found himself holding back a scoff. How could she sleep in a situation like this? His anger was starting to turn into hatred, making him despise every movement she made, every emotion she felt, every word she said. The more time passed, the worse it got and the fact that he kept staring at her with a glare on his face probably only helped the process.

At some point he couldn't stand it anymore. He got up and started walking, forcing his mind to think about anything else. The first person who came to mind was Lucjan, and the hatred in his chest suddenly turned to panic and sadness. If this meeting with the elves was a trap, they would be condemning the kingdom. The civilians would die, and Malkiya would make sure Lucjan followed suit. They shouldn't have wasted time coming here.

"Why do you look so anxious?" Nadzia's annoyance brought him back to reality. "If something happens I'm the only one who won't be able to get out of here alive. You are all fine."

"I'm *angry*," he felt the need to correct her. "We don't have much time left before a whole army of underworld creatures comes to kill everyone in the kingdom and the only allies we might be able to get are refusing to meet us."

He saw from the look in her eyes and the change in her emotions that she understood what he was trying to say.

Her voice was soft when she said, "We'll get back in time."

He had to look away. He couldn't stand the way she'd changed so suddenly. He needed to stay angry at her if he wanted to prevent a disaster.

The sound of the doors opening caught everyone's attention. They were all surprised when the elf soldiers invited them out. Stepping over the threshold, he realised they were in a throne room. The elf king was sitting on his throne on the other side of it, looking completely relaxed.

When Kagen told them to come closer, Xayvion felt a shiver down his spine. The way his voice resounded around the room was not normal. While they walked closer, he looked at them as a predator would his prey.

"You've come in the name of King Lucjan?" Kagen asked.

Xayvion nodded, preparing himself to explain. "Yes. My name is Xayvion. I'm his advisor."

Xayvion realised he actually wasn't the slightest bit ready to meet Kagen when the elf king spoke again.

"Two curious things happened today," Kagen said casually, a small grin making its way onto his face, "First, we have visitors come to us from Phexion of their own accord, secondly, they asked for *me*."

This was all Nadzia's fault. If she hadn't taken over his mind, Xayvion wouldn't have made that stupid little mistake when they'd arrived at the Elf Realm. He should have known better.

He tried to pretend he hadn't understood what Kagen meant, saying instead, "We come with bad news, and a request."

Kagen smiled, intrigued. He leaned forward and told Xayvion to keep talking so he explained the situation, telling Kagen about the attacks on the villages near Lake Naraka, and about Malkiya. He tried to explain how this would be a problem for everyone, including the Elf Realm, and how they could really use the elves' help in fighting Malkiya. But Kagen clearly didn't consider Malkiya a threat since the elves weren't his main target and because they'd be able to fight him with fewer casualties.

"We know we aren't powerful enough alone to fight whatever creatures and demons come for us. Which is why King Lucjan sent us here, to ask for your help," Xayvion finished.

Kagen's look was serious and teasing at the same time. "You want me to give you an army."

"An army, and magical creatures," Xayvion corrected him.

The elf king laughed out loud, amused. "Of course, I forgot how greedy you humans are."

Xayvion had to bite back a retort. He couldn't get on Kagen's bad side now, but his behavior was really getting on Xayvion's nerves. Couldn't he see how critical the situation was? Even if it didn't concern them directly, they did live in the same land.

Having run out of ideas and arguments to try and make him understand, Xayvion ended up asking, "What would convince you to help us?"

Kagen's grin became even bigger. "Well, it would be nice to know how you found out I'm king."

"We heard rumours that your father had died," Xayvion said.

Kagen raised an eyebrow. "That's funny. Because that information has never left my realm."

Xayvion tried to make light of it, hoping this new approach would change things. "You're awfully confident about your men's loyalty."

Unfortunately, however, Kagen's face turned serious and he looked offended. "Unlike you humans, we understand the concept of loyalty perfectly. I would be careful what I say if I were you."

Xayvion had no idea what to do or say anymore. He had been messing things up since they arrived because his mind was already in turmoil, and now he had no way of getting out of the hole he'd dug himself.

Then a thought came to mind— the reminder of a conversation he'd had with Lucjan before they'd left. It only lasted for a brief second, but he forced himself to act on it before he had too much time to consider it carefully.

"We'll give you her," he said, looking straight at Kagen.

He wasn't quick enough to shut out what everyone was feeling, and sensed a huge wave of panic from Nadzia.

"She's the one who told us you were king," he explained quickly, trying to forget about her. He felt her eyes burning holes in the side of his head. "She knows quite a lot of secrets about everyone in this kingdom, you included. All she told us was that your father had died and that you are now the ruler of this realm. If you accept to take her as payment for your help, you'd be able to make sure she doesn't give away any more of your confidential information. And you might learn about other people's secrets, as well."

"That does indeed sound interesting," said Kagen. "I'll take her."

Xayvion should have felt relieved, but instead his heartbeat quickened to match Nadzia's emotions. Her feelings were so loud they invaded all his senses. He felt a ringing in his ears, and an acid taste in his mouth. Everything around him took on shades of purple and red, giving him visual proof of the fear and panic Nadzia was feeling, and he had to close his eyes for a few moments to get back to normal. He had no idea why he was struggling so hard to ignore Nadzia's feelings, but he was finding it very tough indeed.

He heard her plead them to wait, and then he heard her yell his name. The pang in his chest became more and more painful but he convinced himself he was only feeling what she was currently feeling, that those weren't his emotions. When the door shut he almost flinched.

"So, what are the numbers of soldiers you expect me to make available for your army?" Kagen said, nonchalantly, as if he hadn't just forcefully taken a human as prisoner.

Xayvion took a deep breath and tried to look him in the eye while he explained what he and Lucjan had planned. He told him the numbers they needed, the things they would provide, Nadzia's story and everything else Kagen asked. Xayvion kept talking, but his mouth did everything on its own. His mind wasn't there in that room during their discussion, it was deeply lost in guilty thoughts.

✳

Xayvion turned over in bed for the millionth time. He'd been unsuccessfully trying to sleep for hours. His thoughts were so loud he could barely understand what was going on anymore. A voice in his head kept screaming '*Nadzia, Nadzia, Nadzia, Nadzia...*'

His guilt was eating him alive. He'd kept seeing shades of purple and red even after Nadzia wasn't in the same room anymore. He already knew that it was his mind playing tricks on him because there was no way he was actually seeing her emotions from so far away.

Xayvion couldn't get the feeling of her panic out of his head. He felt the way it crushed her as soon as she realised what was happening, as soon as she realised what *he* had done. And the way she had screamed his name, in a last plea for help, would probably haunt him forever.

Now, in the darkness of the bedroom Kagen had made available to him, Xayvion was regretting everything he had done.

Why had he been angry at Nadzia in the first place? Because she wanted to protect herself? Of course she'd kept secrets from them. Just like they couldn't fully trust her, she couldn't fully trust *them*, it was only fair. They had imprisoned her and treated her like a criminal after all.

Even if they still hadn't confirmed her identity, some things about her were sure. She was alone and in a foreign place. All she wanted was to be safe and find a way to return home. Instead of understanding that, Xayvion had given her to an elf king as if she were some sort of prize.

He thought of the way she talked about her home, of the longing and sadness he could always feel from her when she did. He didn't have to use his powers to notice how she often reached out to them, with vulnerability in her eyes and the hope of having someone by her side she could lean on.

"What the hell is wrong with me…" he mumbled to himself, passing a hand over his face.

Would Kagen treat her better than Lucjan? No, that's not possible. Elves are cruel, especially to those who are not like them. Xayvion had probably condemned Nadzia to the worst life possible.

"Shit…"

He jumped off the bed and ran out of the bedroom. There was a guard at the end of the corridor and he rushed towards her.

"I need to see King Kagen," he stated.

The guard was surprised to see him awake and hear his request.

"It's almost dawn, you should wait a few hours," she replied. "You will be seeing him soon anyway."

"No, I need to see him now."

He saw her open her mouth again to reply, but he already knew she was going to say no again so just ignored her and walked off. Her momentary surprise gave him an advantage and he ran down another hallway. He really had no idea where he was going and all the tunnels looked the same, but he knew that these were the sleeping quarters so he wandered around, followed by the guard screaming for him to stop, trying to find anything that would indicate where Kagen was.

When he saw two guards positioned outside a big door, he knew he'd found Kagen's bedroom. The guards had been alarmed by the screaming of the one following Xayvion, and noticed him running towards them from afar. They blocked his path and tried to push him back, but Xayvion made enough noise for everyone to hear.

The door of Kagen's bedroom opened just as one of the guards pointed his sword at Xayvion's neck.

"Stop!"

The three guards and Xayvion halted, all turning to look at Kagen who had clearly been woken up by all the commotion.

"What the hell is going on here?"

One of the guards stepped forward. "He came running towards your bedroom screaming and—"

"I need to speak with you," Xayvion cut him off.

Kagen raised an eyebrow at him, annoyed. "Now?"

"Yes, now."

Kagen sighed, then nodded. He waved his guards away and walked back into his room. Xayvion hurried in after him and closed the door.

"What's so urgent that it couldn't wait til morning?" Kagen asked, sitting on his bed. Despite having been woken by the noise, he looked more tired than annoyed.

"I want to revisit our conditions."

Kagen tilted his head, eyebrow raised, pleasantly surprised.

"I would like to take Nadzia back." Xayvion cringed inside at how the sentence sounded, but needed to make it professional.

"Why? Have you decided you'd like to keep your secrets to yourself?" Kagen jabbed.

Xayvion avoided the question. Instead he said, "Is there anything else you want? Anything else you need? Just name it, and I'll find a way to get it." He looked intensely into Kagen's eyes. "I want Nadzia back."

Kagen studied him silently for a while, and the more time passed the more Xayvion feared he would order the guards to execute him for just trying to go back on the deal. Kagen's expression was serious, but impossible to decipher.

"Why?" He asked.

"Because she's more valuable than I imagined," Xayvion replied, keeping his voice steady and professional.

Kagen, however, wasn't fooled. "To the kingdom, or to you?"

Xayvion was taken back for a second. Would telling the truth be the only way out? Kagen already seemed to have guessed what was actually going on.

Xayvion took a deep breath and gave in. "I made a mistake. I was blinded by anger and feelings of betrayal yesterday and ended up offering you Nadzia as a trade in our deal. I should have protected her and instead I gave up on her as soon as a problem arose." He felt ashamed, but kept his eyes on Kagen to demonstrate he was sincere. "I know I'm not being professional and that there are more important things we should be worrying about, but I need to fix the mess I created. Whatever you want, just name it. I'll give it to you in exchange for Nadzia."

Kagen's silence continued, eating Xayvion alive.

"Please," he said finally, in a whisper.

Kagen got up and walked towards Xayvion, as gracefully as a feline.

"I had the chance to chat with Nadzia for a little while after our meeting yesterday. If you really mean everything you've just said and want to make things right, you'd better work for it." He said, seriously. Xayvion felt so small standing opposite him.

"I do want to make things right," he replied quietly.

Kagen nodded, then walked back to his bed.

"There's nothing I need right now," he stated at last.

Xayvion's heart dropped. "So you won't exchange her for anything?"

"She shouldn't be exchanged," Kagen replied, glaring sternly at him. "She can just be freed."

Xayvion felt his mind was playing tricks on him again. He wasn't sure he understood what was going on.

"I will let Nadzia free, and *she* will decide what to do with her life and where to go from here," Kagen explained. "If she decides to come with us to Phexion, you will have to work for her forgiveness."

"You'll actually free her?" Xayvion asked, in disbelief. "Why?"

Elves were cruel and deceiving, they never did anything for nothing, so why was he so casually saying he would free her?

"She's a nice girl, and deserves a better life than being an oracle or prisoner," Kagen's voice was so sincere that it shocked Xayvion. Even his eyes looked honest.

Maybe the elf king wasn't the kind of person everyone had imagined he was, a thought that made Xayvion's heart feel somewhat lighter.

"She does deserve more," Xayvion confirmed, his voice soft.

There was something weird in the realization that Kagen was being protective over Nadzia, but Xayvion couldn't afford to think about that at the moment. He had hurt Nadzia, and his priority was to make it up to her. He was glad Kagen was giving him the chance to do so.

3.

THE TALK

KAGEN

A confession from Nadzia is not something Kagen ever thought he would hear.

He wasn't used to being interested in others, just as he wasn't used to others showing an interest in him, even just in a friendly way. When Kagen had talked to Nadzia for the first time in the Elf Realm, he'd felt a strange connection with her. Maybe it was the way she seemed to know him so deeply already, or the fact he could feel that she didn't belong in that world with them. She interested him more than he thought possible.

He'd unconsciously started liking Xayvion, too. That had begun the day Xayvion had rushed into his room to ask for Nadzia back. There was something in his eyes, a desperate need to fix the problem he had caused and treat her the way she deserved. Kagen had been so surprised by the look in his eyes because it wasn't one he'd ever seen before. He wanted someone to look like that when thinking of *him*. He wanted *Xayvion* to look like that when thinking of him.

He was aware Nadzia and Xayvion had feelings for each other, it was obvious. Despite his growing fondness for both, Kagen had no intention of acting on it, because he didn't want to get between them. He didn't care that he would be miserable or lonely, as long as the two of them could be happy together. He was content seeing them get closer, and loving them in silence from afar. He was content knowing he had the ability to love at all, something his father had always told him was impossible.

Kagen had tried to support Nadzia, letting her know that if things ever went wrong, or if she didn't feel Phexion was the right place for her, he would be waiting to welcome her with open arms. He hadn't realised that Nadzia felt for him what he felt for her, and that his behavior confused her even more.

When they had had that conversation in the empty dining hall, and she'd told him how she felt, he was both surprised and pleased. When she mentioned choosing between him and Xayvion, all Kagen could think of was '*Why should she choose?*'. He knew he liked both Nadzia *and* Xayvion, so the idea of being able to act on his feelings was exciting. If she also liked both of them, why couldn't all three of them be together?

That night he'd told Nadzia to put the matter aside and focus on the present, that they would worry about it when things were better and they could focus on themselves, but Kagen couldn't wait. He had to hear what Xayvion thought about it all, which was why a few nights later, instead of sleeping as he should have done, he went to look for Xayvion.

He found a soldier leaving her room and rushed to stop her.

"Excuse me," he said politely, "do you know where I can find Xayvion?"

"He should be in his room at his hour," she replied.

"Could you tell me where his room is?"

The soldier pointed him in the right direction. "Last room on the right."

Kagen thanked her and walked to Xayvion's room. The closer he got, the more nervous he felt. He hadn't been afraid when talking with Nadzia, but for some reason he felt scared now that he had to talk to Xayvion.

When he knocked on Xayvion's door, he didn't take long to open it. He looked surprised to see Kagen.

"Can I come in?" Kagen asked.

"Hm, yeah, sure." Xayvion stepped back and let him in, confused by his visit. "Is everything alright?"

"Yes, I just wanted to talk."

"Alright," Xayvion replied cautiously. He gestured for Kagen to follow him to the sofa and they sat down. Xayvion looked at him in silence, waiting for Kagen to start talking.

Kagen's thoughts were a chaotic mess and he hadn't planned far enough ahead to prepare a speech, so when he finally started speaking everything came out all in one go, sounding as messy as he thought it would.

"I like Nadzia," Kagen quickly blurted out, surprising Xayvion even more. "And I like you." Xayvion took a few seconds to process this, but Kagen kept talking before he could find his voice to speak. "I know that you like Nadzia, and I know that Nadzia likes you and that she likes me, too. Explaining it like this sounds like a mess, I know. I talked to her the other day and she was very worried about it all." Kagen said.

Xayvion sighed. "She had the talk with you, too?"

Kagen nodded.

"My feelings for Nadzia grow each passing minute, but I know I'm not alone in her heart," Xayvion said. He sounded a little defeated. "She keeps a place for you, too."

Kagen looked at him carefully. "And that bothers you?"

"Yes," he admitted. "I don't know if I'm scared of losing her or if I'm just selfish, but I don't like the fact that I'm not the only one."

"Why would you be scared of losing her?" Kagen asked, genuinely curious.

Xayvion looked at him as if he were out of his mind, as if Kagen couldn't begin to understand what he meant.

"Because she might end up choosing you." His eyes looked sad when he said it. "She might realise that she didn't really like me, that I'm not enough for her, or that she simply prefers you. She might slip away and disappear from my life just to be with you."

"Why should there be a choice?" Kagen asked. He could understand Xayvion's fear, but he couldn't understand why he hadn't thought of another option. "It doesn't have to be one or the other."

Xayvion frowned. "What do you mean?"

"We both like her, and she likes both of us, so why can't we both be with her?" Kagen said, adding quickly, "Don't get me wrong, I don't mean to say we should share her, like I imagine you're thinking right now. I mean to say we could, all three of us, be together."

Xayvion didn't really seem to understand what he was trying to say.

Kagen pointed to himself and asked, "Can you see yourself liking me in the future? Can you see yourself being attracted to me?"

Xayvion studied Kagen as if he were seeing at him for the first time. He was pensive for a few seconds, then replied, "I'm not sure. You're a good person and I can't deny you're good looking. I can't say it won't happen, but I can't guarantee it will, either."

"That's enough for me. If there's even a small chance, I can work with that," Kagen said, giving him a small smile. "You can't choose who to fall in love with, but you can eventually choose who to love."

Finally, Xayvion seemed to catch up with everything he had been saying until then.

"So what you're saying is that there could be three of us in a relationship?"

Kagen nodded. "That way we don't have to feel guilty or worry about each other's feelings. We can act however we want with Nadzia because we'd both have the right to do so, and she could act the same with us. As I said earlier, I like you, so I'd love to be able to act that way with you too someday, but for the moment I won't do anything unless you tell me it's okay. I don't want to force you to like me back. I just want you to know that if some day you feel like closing the last point of the triangle, I'd be happy about it."

"What if we do this and one day she realises she likes you more and that she'd rather only be with you?" Xayvion repeated his worry, his voice quiet. "I don't think I'd be able to handle that. I don't want to lose her to someone else."

"I think you should have a little more faith in Nadzia's feelings," Kagen replied softly.

Xayvion looked away, biting his lip out of nervousness.

"I'm not sure about this," he said. "The idea of both being with her sounds like a good *and* a bad idea at the same time."

"You don't have to give me an answer now," Kagen added quickly to reassure him. "As I said to her, at the moment we have other things to worry about. A war is about to happen and we can't afford to focus on personal matters."

"You're right, we should be focusing on other things." Xayvion nodded, frowning.

Kagen wanted to reach out to Xayvion to comfort him physically, by holding his hand or putting an arm around his shoulder but didn't want to make him feel uncomfortable, especially now that it seemed like he was making progress.

"Just consider it, think about whether it might be something you could find yourself trying, so when the war is over, all three of us can discuss it."

Xayvion ran a hand through his hair, nervously. "What do we do in the meantime? How do we behave around Nadzia?"

"Would it be okay for you if we both act the way we want to act? If we want to give her space we do that, if we want to hold her then we hold her with no hard feelings. Just being ourselves around her without any competition. I guess we could see it as a trial period, in order to understand if you're comfortable with that kind of situation."

Xayvion bit his lip again, lost in thought. Slowly, he started nodding. "Okay, we can try that."

"If you realise you're not comfortable with it, you should tell me so I can back off," Kagen said in a serious tone. "The most important thing to me is how you two feel, and I don't want to make either of you unhappy."

Xayvion's eyes softened at that. "Thank you."

Kagen smiled back at him. They looked into each other's eyes in silence for a while, but since neither of them had anything more to say, Kagen stood up. Xayvion stood up as well and quietly walked with him to the door.

"Kagen?"

The elf king stopped and turned towards him.

"I won't be in Phexion tomorrow," Xayvion started. "Could you take care of Nadzia for me?"

Kagen smiled softly. The fact that Xayvion was willingly asking him to get closer to Nadzia, even if for just one day and just this occasion, was already a big step.

"Of course."

Xayvion smiled back, shyly. "Thank you."

The two said goodbye for the night and Kagen walked back to his room, a feeling of relief washing over him. The talk had gone better than he'd expected and despite what Xayvion had said, his eyes and body language told Kagen that he might eventually agree to what he had proposed. All Kagen had to do was be patient, but that was fine. He had all the time in the world to wait.

4.

THE AFTERMATH

KAGEN

Kagen regretted telling Nadzia it was okay for her to break his heart.

Of course, it had been worth it. He would never regret meeting her and would be forever grateful to her for showing him he was capable of loving and being loved, enabling him to meet amazing people and letting him know that it was okay to be himself instead of pretending to be someone else.

The fact was that when he said what he had about her breaking his heart, he'd thought it might happen because she'd chosen to be with Xayvion instead of both of them, or because she'd had to go home. He hadn't thought for a second she would break his heart by dying.

The sight of her, covered in blood, laying in Xayvion's arms unable to move, smiling at them and repeating over and over that everything was okay… That was a sight Kagen would never forget, one that haunted him in his nightmares and also when he was awake, once he'd realized it had really happened.

He had wanted to stay in Phexion at first, to feel closer to Nadzia in any way possible, but after the funeral the memories hurt too much, and he chose to return to the Elf Realm and act as a king again. Pretending to be composed was hard. Fixing his face so his eyes didn't show his grief was even harder.

His soldiers realised he was grieving, but they didn't know who he was grieving for. He felt guilty when he told them, as an excuse, that he felt sorry for all the soldiers that had died in battle. They believed him without a second thought, which only made Kagen feel worse.

He tried to keep in touch with the friends he'd eventually made in Phexion. Xayvion wrote him letters, usually to discuss how they were both doing and how they were handling the loss. Dacey and Lucjan also wrote occasionally to ask how he was doing or if he would be visiting them again one day. Lucjan had told Kagen he was welcome to go there whenever he wanted, but he had never replied. He wasn't sure going back to Phexion would be good for him.

Months after Nadzia's funeral, Xayvion visited the Elf Realm.

Kagen was thrilled at the idea of seeing him again, thinking the sight of someone he cared about would comfort him, but instead he felt his heart drop as soon Xayvion arrived. Seeing his face, he couldn't help but realise how much he had missed him in the past months. Right after that, the feeling of sadness turned to pure heartache, reminding Kagen of what he had lost. Of *who* both of them had lost.

Kagen still wanted to hold Xayvion in his arms, but without Nadzia it felt like a piece was missing. And while he knew Xayvion wanted to make sure he was alright, he knew he wasn't ready to accept him in that way— not yet, anyway.

Kagen's memory of that meeting was a bit blurry. He remembered Xayvion telling him Nadzia showed herself and that he was so shocked he made Xayvion repeat the sentence multiple times. Xayvion explained how she had appeared to them, that she was alive and safe in her world. Kagen had fallen to his knees in relief at the news, but his feelings of joy didn't last long. Xayvion told him Nadzia had wanted to see him, that she had tried to, but hadn't been able to. He told Kagen she was sorry, like Nadzia had asked him to.

Xayvion stayed in the Elf Realm for a few days after that, but Kagen spent those days in misery in his room. He cried in his sleep, which irritated him, and when he was awake and his mind betrayed him with all the memories, the tears wouldn't fall, and that irritated him even more.

He was glad to know Nadzia was alive and safe, but the fact he had been told about it and hadn't been there to find out personally made it sound like a lie in his head. Yes, Nadzia was safe, but was she really? It made getting over her death even harder.

It took Kagen a few weeks to recover from Xayvion's visit. One day he woke up and forced himself to find a new purpose. The new purpose ended up being research.

He spent all his time studying and reading everything he could get his hands on about travels between worlds. He compared Nadzia's story with the ones he managed to find, trying to find similarities and possible clues.

XAYVION

It was another few months before Xayvion visited Kagen again. Obsessed with his studying, Kagen hadn't replied to his last few letters, which worried Xayvion.

When he arrived at the Elf Realm, the soldiers let him in without any problem, now knowing he was a friend. He tried asking about Kagen, but the elves avoided eye contact and ignored his questions. Xayvion's anxiety grew by the second, and when he finally opened the door to Kagen's bedroom, his heart skipped a beat.

The bed, the desk and most of the floor were covered in books, papers and scrolls in more languages than Xayvion could possibly recognize. Kagen was walking back and forth, mumbling things under his breath and repeatedly running a hand through his already messy hair.

"Kagen…" Xayvion said softly.

He had meant to whisper it to himself, but somehow Kagen still heard him. When he turned and noticed Xayvion standing in the room, his eyes lit up, but not in the way Xayvion would have liked. Kagen ran over and put his hands on his shoulders, dragging him inside his room with him.

"Look what I found," he said.

His tone was supposed to be enthusiastic, but it made Xayvion's blood chill. Kagen picked up a book and showed it to him.

"Look at this, it says that some day around two thousand years ago the tribes that lived on this land used to travel between worlds, which is how this land came to be inhabited by so many different species and kinds of people." He was pointing at something in the book, but Xayvion couldn't take his eyes off Kagen, who was surrounded by a yellow aura and looked possessed. This wasn't the Kagen he knew. What had happened since the last time he'd seen him?

Xayvion took the book from his hands and closed it, dropping it onto the bed next to them. Kagen frowned at him in confusion.

"What are you doing?" He asked, his voice shaking with nervousness. "I was showing you something important."

"I know," Xayvion replied.

Kagen unconsciously raised his voice. "That could be the key to seeing Nadzia again, can't you see it's important?"

Xayvion opened his mouth to reply but Kagen cut him off before he could try. "I thought you loved her too. Don't you want to see her again? You saw her after she died! You saw her and I didn't and I won't believe what you said until I see it for myself! I can't know if she's alright unless I see her myself. Don't you want to see her?"

His sentences were broken, sometimes they didn't belong to the same train of thought and sometimes he repeated the same one again and again. Xayvion felt his heart break as he listened to Kagen talk, but the sight became too painful to watch and he felt the need to do something.

He took Kagen's face between his hands and forced him to stop and look directly at him.

"It's not impossible," Kagen continued. "There's a way to meet her again. There's a way to connect our worlds. We could—"

"Breathe," Xayvion ordered him calmly. "Kagen, breathe."

"But—"

"Breathe… Please."

Kagen looked at Xayvion with a shocked expression for a few moments, as if he couldn't understand why he was acting that way. Xayvion waited patiently and looked at him intensely until Kagen gave in and tried to calm down, taking deep breaths, never breaking eye contact.

"You're hurting yourself like this," Xayvion told Kagen softly. "When was the last time you got a good night's sleep? Or the last time you ate? You've lost so much weight since my last visit."

Kagen's voice was quiet and ashamed when he replied, "I didn't have time…"

Xayvion sighed. "Nadzia would want you to take care of yourself."

Kagen flinched at the mention of her name.

"I miss her too, you know? I would love to see her one more time, and I understand how *you* must feel, having her dead body laying in front of you as your last memory of her." Xayvion said, quietly. "We've tried to deal with the loss in our own ways, and we're both a mess right now." Xayvion wasn't acting like Kagen, but he knew he didn't look well either. He couldn't deny that. Finally, he said, "Let me take care of you. If we can't deal with this on our own, let's do it together. I don't need to go back to Phexion, I can stay here with you."

Kagen's eyes were wide and teary, his voice shaking. "You'd stay with me?"

"Yes."

Kagen's arms enveloped Xayvion in a tight, desperate hug. He hid his face in the crook of Xayvion's neck and only then did he realise how hard Kagen was shaking.

"Do you think it will ever get better?" Kagen asked quietly, his breath tickling Xayvion's neck.

"It will, but it will also take time," Xayvion replied, hugging him back. "We'll need time."

That, surprisingly, seemed to be enough for Kagen. He relaxed into Xayvion who held him for as long as he needed. He knew Nadzia would be glad to see them helping each other, and that thought made him smile for the first time in a long while.

ACKNOWLEDGEMENTS

I must thank quite a few people this time around, too.

First of all, thanks to the TikTok community of readers and fellow authors, for your support and always hyping me up.

Thanks to my amazing beta readers, especially Tasha, Lily, Ella, Kaitlynn and Jenn who have been extremely helpful. This story would be so much duller without your advice.

Thank you Carman and Vasilisa, for putting up with me when I tried to make sense of my thoughts and explain how I wanted the artwork. You deserve an award for your immense patience.

Last but not least, thank YOU reader for picking up this book. It all started with a random thought I had in the middle of the night and I hope I've managed to turn it into something you were able to enjoy.

Make sure you follow Carman and Vasilisa and check out their other artwork!

Carman:
instagram & twitter & tumblr & tiktok: @cchaiart

Vasilisa:
instagram: @padrebasil.art // twitter & tiktok: @padrebasil

ABOUT
THE AUTHOR

Margherita Scialla (she/they) is a gen-z author born and raised in Italy. She obsessively studied languages for years, only to drastically change paths and study design at university.

They now spend their days procrastinating and avoiding all and any responsibility (and getting her driving license) in order to read and write.

www.margheritascialla.com

tiktok & instagram: @themargherita.s

OTHER BOOKS BY MARGHERITA SCIALLA

What The Stars Didn't Show Us

"Life isn't easy when you have a brother who's always considered better than you. Hyunsuk's situation is even worse since he shares the same face as his so-called perfect twin. His life starts to change, however, when a new student arrives at his school and she sees something in him no one else had ever bothered to look for.

Hialeah, already too familiar with the feeling of being alone, is set on befriending him, but can Hyunsuk finally come out of his twin's shadow and open up to someone, when his brother makes it clear he doesn't want him to find happiness?"

Printed in Great Britain
by Amazon

80949826R10176